STEALING SAINTS

A BLACK ORCHID ENTERPRISES MYSTERY
BOOK 6

M. R. DIMOND

*Dedicated to those whose holidays
hold more tears than joy
and to the memory of
Nigel, Sphynx cat extraordinaire*

FOREWORD

Thanks for joining me on another adventure. If you need to refresh your memory on who's who, see the Cast of Characters at the end of the book.

JD Thompson

PROLOGUE

Because it was beginning to look a lot like Christmas, that magical season (including more than a hundred other holidays), I hid in the warmth of the Beauchamp Cat Shelter, housed in a former barn behind Gregg House. Very Christmassy, though the barn-shelter contained no mangers. After the parking areas emptied, I braved the cold and pulled my suit jacket tight across my chest, for all the good that did against the frigid Texas air.

I dashed across the backyard, pushing a cartful of cat crates in front of me. Law school did not cover this situation. I rattled up the ramp to the Gregg House vet clinic's back door. Over the clattering wheels and crates, eleven cats screamed in a disjointed chorus with the clinic cats, all sure death was imminent.

When I shoved my burden through the door between clinic and house, I glanced down the long gallery and saw only two of my house-mates at the far end. Life, for the moment, was good, even though a Sphynx cat stuck a paw through the crate bars and snagged my ear with his fishhook-sized claws.

My dress shoes on the wood floor added to the noise as I labored toward the front door. The party food from our all-city, all-county, half-of-Texas holiday open house had vanished, but the aromas lingered. Pumpkin Spice season had sloshed into Chocolate Peppermint season, with support from five cultures—Jewish, Asian, Desi, Mexican, and my own plain old American.

Once I pushed past the kitchen and serving tables, the scent of winter evergreens, twisted into wreaths and sprays, stomped the lingering traces of sugar and spice. Wreaths and garlands adorned every surface and wall in the Mega-Maxi-Dickensian holiday decor. I swerved around the T-Rex-sized Christmas tree that reached for the heavens, or at least the second floor, of this cathedral-like hall. The cats objected. Metal screeched and clanked.

The Gregg House living room, down the gallery-hall from the kitchen, clinic, and stairs, gave off its gracious mid-twentieth-century vibe with a semicircle of velvety chairs and sofa. Discreet dark wooden end tables nestled close to them. The chairs could easily turn to face the fire or the opposite wall where a large-screen TV hid behind a Vietnamese tapestry of yellow silk painted with rollicking red cats, one of the décor surprises that honored Johnny's now-deceased Vietnamese grandfather. He'd come to the US with Johnny's Jewish grandmother after her stint as a nurse in the Vietnam war.

The most beautiful woman in the world, Dianne Cortez, my three-time ex-girlfriend and current business partner, had arranged herself artistically on the 1940s gold velvet sofa, which complemented her flared green velour party dress. She trimmed it with new red accessories every year. Her wavy black hair had tumbled out of its updo and hung over a sofa arm, but at my approach, she raised herself up and ran to the crates.

"Oh, good. You brought in the house cats. I wondered where you were." She pulled a golden flame-point Siamese from captivity and snuggled her cat to her cheek.

Johnny Ly, my other partner, remarked, "With all the recent trauma, I didn't like to leave the cats unguarded. JD and I have been trading off staying with them this afternoon."

Johnny, of course, has always needed time away from parties, even his own. Me? Dianne raised first one, then a second skeptical, eyebrow.

Johnny perched on the throne-like red velvet chair from the same era as the sofa. During his grandmother's fifty-year reign, she sat there and ruled over us and all Beauchamp. Though she'd retired and turned the house over to Johnny, he looked more like a kid sitting with the grownups for the first time, a weird observation when he'd completed vet school and most of a zoo vet residency.

Mrs. Ly had started the open house tradition over fifty years ago to let people eat and gawk at her historic mansion. She used the occasion to introduce us to the community when Johnny and his college buddies and bandmates (MultiABBA, still available for hire) ditched our urban professional jobs and moved to Beauchamp to treat cats, work accountancy magic, and practice law.

Now that we're introduced to the town, I've no idea why we keep throwing these extravaganzas, except that the population of Central Texas would still show up on our doorstep on the third Saturday of December.

Dianne's eyebrows still hovered around her hairline. I responded with my sweetest smile, not as effective with her these days.

She lifted one shoulder in a mini-shrug and returned to the sofa, the tableau now enhanced by the Siamese on her chest, rising and falling with her breath. "JD, do you realize this is the first open house we've given without a murder?"

"The party is technically over, but the night is young," Johnny observed as he helped me release the cats, those who normally lived in the house but who had been banished to the shelter for the party.

Reactions ranged from pressing against the crate and refusing to come out (the newer residents, kittens waiting on their adoptions) to climbing into my arms (Havoc,* the black-and-white cow cat who'd claimed me), and to darting out like a rocket. Rocket Cat would be Godzilla the Sphynx, † searching for his owner Chantal Gaumont, already at the restaurant with our families.

I shifted Havoc to answer my phone at its command. I sighed at the text summons. "Somebody, quick. Invite me over for Christmas."

Dianne frowned. "I don't think I can, JD. My sister Lourdes just got engaged. My mother would flip out, thinking we were next. She's thrilled about Lourdes, of course, but she can't look at me without crying."

---

* Havoc claimed me in *Hallow: A Fractured Family Tale*, Book 5

† Godzilla found us in *The Sphynx Who Stole Christmas*, Book 2.

Johnny considered. "Do you want to come with my family to Uncle Phan's on Christmas Day?"

Havoc and the phone were too much to handle. I let her jump down to swat her kittens into submission. "Thanks, Johnny. Possibly, but I need a good excuse to bail on my family. They once again sent me the Thompson family Christmas plans. They know I never read them until after this bash, hence the late invitation. This year my father's hosting the whole family—grandparents, aunts, cousins, and random strangers—at my childhood home he keeps threatening to sell. 'One last gathering.' Ha."

"Why is that a problem?" Dianne tried to run her fingers through her snarled hair after one of the kittens jumped in it. In ancient times, I might have gently brushed out the tangles for her. Now she'd stuff the brush down my throat.

"His co-host. Hostess." I paused to get my voice under control. "Mallory."*

"Mallory," repeated Dianne.

Johnny whispered, "Mallory."

Mallory. The lovely librarian lady, my newly discovered step aunt or similar, but—this is important—not a biological relative. I fell in love at first sight; she, not so much. Not with me anyway. She thought I was a kid, too young for a forty-something woman, even though my next birthday is the big 3-0. But when she met my dad at Thanksgiving ...

Dianne shook her head. "You're supposed to go to the home where you grew up, where your parents lived together, and spend Christmas Day with your dad and his new girlfriend, who happens to be your old girlfriend?"

"Wannabe girlfriend," I corrected. "Wannabe on my side."

"Still."

"Even I can see the social difficulties," Johnny volunteered with a proud smile, relieved to see what the problem was.

I leaned back and closed my eyes. "I'll send virtual presents with regrets. I just need a halfway decent excuse to skip out."

Dianne responded with furrowed brow. "I don't know. The nuns

---

* For Mallory's story, see *Hallow: A Fractured Family Tale*, Book 5

used to tell us the way to deal with moral dilemmas was to ask, 'Who would it hurt?'"

"The nuns you always despised? The nuns of the church you never attended in college except when at your family's home for the holidays?"

"She attends once a month now," Johnny said.

I snorted, remembering Dianne spewing curses as she left the house for Mass. "Only because her mother made friends with all the Latinas in Beauchamp, and they'd report her if she didn't show up in church regularly."

Dianne pulled herself up to her full, almost-six-foot height, or length, given her current position. "Whatever my beliefs or feelings, I hope I am one to give credit where it's due, and taking inventory of possible damage seems a good basis for morality."

"I'm in the clear then. Who *would* it hurt if I didn't show up for Christmas presents and dinner?" I sighed down to my shoes, the dress shoes pinching my feet. I hardly ever wear them in these glory days when Casual Friday is every day I don't go to court. "You mean my sisters, don't you?"

"JD, I am neither your moral preceptor nor your priest. But since you asked, did you not notice Merry* during the party?"

"Not really."

Dianne aimed a sword-sharp gaze at me. "Not really, because you did your best to never spend more than thirty seconds with anyone. Merry is pregnant, and she is fragile."

Checking out of this fight, Johnny gazed at the frescoed ceiling while tabbies Gilly and Ginger competed for his lap.

I scooped up a couple of Havoc's kittens and dropped into one of the gold armchairs. "She and Cherry are going to Houston with my grandparents tomorrow or the next day. I'll talk to her before then, maybe at Casa Gracias tonight. Speaking of which, shouldn't we go join everyone else there?"

Over the years, we started collapsing for a short time after the guests left our holiday party while our event workers, also known as family, repaired to the local Mexican restaurant. The first time, a semi-police

---

* For Merry's story, see *Family Matters: Lies Across Texas*, Book 3

dog wouldn't let us leave. Later, we realized it was nice to have time to regroup between events.

A shriek came from a nearby bedroom.

I started in surprise and looked over at my sister Merry in the doorway. She looked like a small tank topped with the Thompson family fluffy blonde curls.

Her sky-blue eyes widened in terror. "I was taking a nap and your horrible cat jumped on me, the one that looks like a gigantic rat or maybe a bat."

"Godzilla," we three chorused.

"He's harmless," said Dianne.

"Mostly harmless," I corrected, remembering the time Johnny drove our intern to the ER after Godzilla bit him. "I thought you went to the restaurant with the rest of the fam. Are you feeling okay?"

She rubbed her arms. "I'm just tired. I took a nap for the last hour of the party. Are you coming home for Christmas?"

Abandoning all hope of escape, I said, "Sure. I'll come for Christmas dinner, maybe a little earlier for presents. Do you want to go to Casa Gracias tonight for the after-party?" If the answer was no, I was staying home with her. She looked peaked. Mentally I calculated how long it would take to get Merry to the nearest hospital.

"Tomorrow I'll make cranberry-orange mashup for you to contribute," Johnny promised.

Merry sighed. "I'll get my coat, though it only goes halfway around me."

"I'll drive us." With a last nuzzle on her cat's nose, Dianne stood up.

I picked up my phone and frowned at the contact notification from my work webpage.

JESSA THORNTON

Hello, are you the JD Thompson who was my stepbrother Nick's friend in high school? I'm trying to reach him about urgent family matters. If you're in touch with him, could you give him my contact information and let him know I need to talk with him as soon as possible? Best, Jessa Thornton

I groaned, an automatic reaction to my friend's bratty little sister who followed us around, insisting on being included in whatever we were doing. Jessa's stepfather, Nick's father, must have adopted her, since she now shared Nick's surname. But she still called Nick her stepbrother. Interesting, but I wasn't remotely tempted to wade into the toxic swamp called the Thornton family. I sent Jessa a brief message.

JD THOMPSON

Jessa, I haven't talked to Nick in many years, but I'll pass your message along if I happen to hear from him. Cordially, JD Thompson

Then I blasted a text to my Houston friends' list, mostly dormant for the ten years after I left Houston for college in Austin.

JD THOMPSON

Happy Whatever of Whichever Season You Celebrate. I need to bail on an overload of family on Christmas Day. Does anybody have an emergency that only I can help with, say early afternoon, after the last bite of pumpkin pie?

It was my last hope.

CHAPTER 1

Christmas arrived, like it does. The dawn's early light saw me scooping litter boxes with Johnny and setting out food for our shelter full of cats, those in Johnny's clinic, and our house cats, now up to eleven with the addition of harlequin-patterned Havoc and her four kittens.

Litter boxes suited my mood. Our intern, the Scooper in Chief, was spending the holidays with his family. Dianne had taken off for Dallas the Sunday afternoon after our open house (the better to avoid Mass with the family). I knew she wouldn't last until New Year's, but at least she would be a Good Daughter and help prepare for the holidays. That left me as the one Johnny could count on for cat duty until the new year settled in.

With the sky sulky and the air cold, close to freezing, I set out for Houston with car heater and music system blasting. From Beauchamp to the Thompson home on Rice Boulevard takes two standard Taylor Swift albums, sandwiched between two ten-minute "All Too Wells." As Taylor moaned the last "all too well," I parked on the street and killed the ignition. I checked my phone, any excuse to delay. I was in for a full day of family, a word high on my personal list of F-words, no friend having responded to my plea from last Saturday before I left Beauchamp.

Feeling the opposite of anxious to join the family debacle inside, I scrolled through my phone. In a Christmas miracle, I found a text from an old friend.

NICK THORNTON

> JD, if you still want something to do this afternoon, could you come get me and my service dog? Bernie gave me until New Year's to get out, but I can't stand it anymore. My car died and I don't have any way to leave.

That would be Jessa's stepbrother Nick, my friend from high school and Scouts. Nick, who lived in my house part of senior year because his family threw him out. He came to my mother's funeral and wept like he was her son. (Her son sat like a crumbling statue behind the floral arrangements.)

I hadn't exchanged words with Nick in years. He was always working on the rare occasions I was in Houston and reached out on my old friends' chat. This week not only did I hear from him but his stepsister, part of the family that cast him out.

I never knew exactly why. He'd called himself bisexual since age twelve. His mother had left the same year, and his father remarried several years later. He'd been dating a girl—Angela? Angelica?—several years after that when his family broke up with him. His girlfriend did too.

I didn't know much about his family situation. Nick didn't either on that long ago winter night when he showed up at our scout meeting in tears, blubbering the bare facts and a lot of Why? Why? Why? After a quick call to my mother, I told him he could come home with me. Mother, of course, took him under her wing. Dad wasn't as excited, but that was normal. They both talked with Nick's parents but went tightlipped after those conversations. Mother assured Nick he could stay as long as he wanted.

Neither Nick nor I learned any more about his parents' reasons. Our best guess was his sexual orientation, but why would it be a problem at age seventeen, five years after he came out?

We double-dated for Prom, marched across the graduation stage together (Thompson, Thornton). We planned to room together at the University of Texas, but he bailed on me at the last minute. Instead he went to community college to avoid drowning in debt. I was mad at the time, but since my roommate turned out to be sixteen-year-old Johnny, I can't say it didn't work out for me.

The cold seeping through to my skin brought me back to the fa-la-la-la present. I looked up to see my relatives peering out of and tapping on the living room windows. I sent Nick a quick text.

JD THOMPSON

Sure. Deets?

Draping my coat over Johnny's cranberry goo, I ran toward the front door, gasping in the icy air. It's a Southern thing, taking a coat but not putting it on. If you do put it on, you don't zip or button it. Then you complain about how cold it is.

I visited relatives in Massachusetts one Christmas, and they laughed when I realized (1) that I had to put on my jean jacket, (2) that I had to snap it shut, and (3) that a jean jacket was humorously inadequate in the snowy North. The cousins took me shopping and bought me a hooded puffy coat. No one had to tell me again to snap it shut before stepping outdoors. Now that same coat protected Johnny's cranberry-orange mess. The coat still looked good after most of a decade because I didn't need it more than a day or two in Texas winters.

A massive evergreen wreath bulged out of the front door like a tumor. A cousin pulled the door open as I climbed the two stairs to the stoop, with the words "all too well" still thrumming in my brain.

As the heat from inside the house exploded in my face, I sighed in relief that my first worst nightmare did not come to pass. Mallory didn't greet me at the door as hostess. I don't know who opened the door; the house was stuffed to overflowing with every Thompson connection I'd ever met and some I swear I hadn't.

Someone had turned the heat to the highest setting, Death of a Sun, and lit a fire in the fireplace. Having gone from toasty warm car to frigid outdoors to baking temps inside the house, my exposed skin cells gave notice to quit. I felt like Hansel and Gretel had pushed me into the witch's oven.

The smells of fifty people's special holiday dishes, tinted with pine and spruce holiday scents, clogged the air and helped with the oven metaphor. No doubt each dish would be delicious, but my nostrils joined my skin in resigning. I plowed through my nearest but not dearest as everyone shouted greetings. "How are you, JD?" "Been a while, JD" "Whatcha up to these days?" "Sure is cold," et effing cetera.

Someday I'll test my theory that I could say absolutely anything in response and no one would notice. I'll start with "It's Jaymey now—having my surgery next week," "Glad I could make bail," "I'm in remission," "Rehab let me go for the day," "Leaving for my Peace Corps destination tomorrow." But because my specific goal for the day was enduring a few hours here without a ruckus, I let traditional responses grease my way to the kitchen, where I encountered Mallory.

Her pretty, freckled face was flushed from the heat and smudged with samples of all the delicacies. My heart went boom as it fell to the floor and shattered one more time.

"I'm glad you're here, JD." She wiped her face with the edge of her apron, as grubby as her face. "I wanted to talk to you at your open house, but I never caught up with you."

I thrust Johnny's dish at her in a defensive motion. An aunt or cousin—the kitchen was full of them—whisked my coat away. I hoped I could find it later. I recalled from deep memory how to smile. "You know how it is when you're the host. Always moving."

She lifted the lid and took a deep sniff of the tart cranberries and tangy citrus. "That's lovely. Does it need to go in the oven?" She glanced doubtfully as an aunt shoved in a pan of rolls on top of the oven's contents.

I backed out of the room, stepping on a small cousin in the process. I raised my voice over the wails. "It's already baked. Warming it by any means should be fine. It's good cold too. I've eaten it for breakfast."

Flashing a ghost of a smile, she turned to survey the possibilities—standard oven, microwave, convection oven, warming trays. I took my chance to dash toward my next obligation: sisters.

CHAPTER 2

Eel-like, I slithered through the crowd. I paused by the polished walnut baby grand piano as my grandmother rippled through "Carol of the Bells." I can't remember any family function that Grandmother didn't spend at the piano, unless she was ill.

I put an arm around her shoulders and pressed my cheek against her soft, white hair. "You ought to play 'Lawyers in Love.' You'll never have a better audience for it."

Her eyes twinkled, and she obliged with the last line of the chorus. A few people looked around, puzzled, but most kept up their chatter, a competitive sport for a family of eighty percent lawyers. "How do you know that fine old song, JD?"

"It's my intro song, the one the band plays after 'and on keyboards and vocals, JD Thompson, attorney at laaaaaaaaaaaw.'"

She laughed and moved into Ralph Vaughn Williams' "Greensleeves." Grandmother had given piano lessons to all her children, nieces, nephews, and grandchildren. She's pleased that I still perform, even in an ABBA tribute band.

"JD!" My sister Cherry pounced and grabbed my arm. "We've been waiting for you to open our prezzies."

Modern presents tend to be air and electrons: money in your account or an old-fashioned check, a gift card to an online or brick-and-mortar location, tickets to some experience. My sisters and I could huddle on Mother's vintage couch with its cream and blue jacquard stripes and embroidered flowers and exchange paper and cards, though I'd made an effort to get a few real things to open. They had too.

Cherry perched on the wooden arm next to Merry and glared the guests away, like a guardian lioness, while we opened presents in record time, a heart-aching contrast to the days when the room held a massive Scotch pine tree and wall-to-wall Barbies and bikes. Mother had sat in Merry's place with legs tucked under her, eager to see us enjoy our bounty. I sat on Merry's other side, angling my gaze away from the unpleasantly warm fire. A few months ago I'd been trapped in a burning building, and I no longer wanted to see chestnuts or anything else roasting on an open fire.

In contrast, we murmured thanks to each other. I actually meant them. My sisters' college-student budgets meant I had a fine collection of fidget toys and Japanese tchotchkes. But Cherry gave me a collection of cat toys that my cat Havoc and her babies would appreciate. Merry, a gifted artist, had painted a watercolor of Havoc and her family from the photo I sent my sisters when the cats came to live in my bedroom.

I handed each twin a hefty-sized gift bag (one magenta, one turquoise), big enough to hold a week's worth of trash or dirty laundry. Merry's mouth formed a silent O as she held up a cornflower blue velour robe the size of a patio umbrella. She clutched it to her heart.

"What's not for her to like?" asked Cherry as she shook her own robe loose. "It's blue, it matches her eyes, it's trimmed with smocking, lace, and little satin flowers—"

"And it just might go all the way around me." Holding the opposite edges of the garment, Merry held her arms straight out. The robe still sagged in the middle.

Cherry liked her slimmer, cherry-colored robe too, not surprising, since Dianne picked it out. The contrast between the identical twins broke my heart. As curly-headed blonde tots, they were adorable. So I'm told. Born when I was nine to a mother who soon suffered from cancer, I babysat them more than any of us would have liked.

As they grew, Cherry straightened and chopped her hair into angles while Merry kept the curls and softness. Now, Cherry was as mean and lean as ever (with a maroon rinse in her short hair for the holidays), but Merry looked heavy, swollen, and exhausted.

She never glowed in this pregnancy, as some people, mostly novelists say, but I wouldn't expect a young woman pregnant by sexual assault to glow about anything ever. No one wanted her to bear this child, but she set her soft chin in granite-like determination. Her body, her choice, her rules, as I frequently said to our father since the full horror of her experience burst on us.

I turned my attention back to the gifts, now predictable, but still welcome. A CD from the latest Tchaikovsky Prize winner, because Grandmother hasn't grasped streaming yet. A subscription to an over-priced online legal reference from my grandfather, who has made the transition from paper and knows how much even electrons cost, especially for a young lawyer in his own practice. The gift-wrapped box from my father looked thick for his standard check.

As a shadow fell across us, the three of us pressed together, all thinking, "I am so grounded for life," our standard reaction to being confronted by the man looming over us.

"Cherry, don't sit on the arm of the couch," our father admonished.

She made a face and plopped down on the other side of me while I tore into Dad's gift. Removing the last of the paper revealed two slim collections of poetry, one by the young poet Amanda Gorman, the other by Joy Harjo, current US poet laureate.

"Mallory said you'd like those books," he said to me.

"She was right," I said, pulling out the check that stuck out from Ms. Harjo's work. From the amount, I must have offended him even more than usual this year. I teased out a printout from Ms. Gorman's "The Hill We Climb."

Dad cleared his throat. "I didn't want to buy that without knowing whether you'd want it, but if you'd like to go to a poetry or music workshop this next year, I'm willing to fund it."

I gawked at the printout. Merry shoved my jaw shut.

"Mallory heard good things about that poetry workshop in Scotland." Dad folded his arms across his chest. His speech sounded rehearsed, but not enough. "You'll want to do your own research and pick the best event for you, but it's not too early to check into them. You might have to send samples of your work."

"I really—I can't tell you how—this will be great." I struggled to untangle my tongue. My father? *Buying* me something I'd like?

"He's sending me to Hollywood for acting classes," whispered Cherry, awed. "After graduation."

Merry managed a smile. "And I'll let him know where I want to go and when I can do anything besides take care of a baby."

"We'll help you do things nearby at least, though Paris might have to wait." My phone buzzed against my rear with a text message. Checking it gave me an escape from gratitude on loop. "Hey, you guys remember Nick Thornton?"

"Emergency backup brother in y'all's senior year." Cherry examined the tags on her robe.

"How is Nick?" My father was going to break his face if he kept up this imitation of a human being.

"Not good. He quit his job to follow love across the country, but his partner broke up with him, and now he's jobless and homeless. He wants me to come help him move out."

Merry's eyes filled with tears. "That's sad."

"It is. If he needs a place to stay for a few days, he can come back here," said my father, not exactly choking on the words.

I thought about yelling, "What have you done with my dad?" Honestly, though, Pod Dad was an improvement.

CHAPTER 3

Everyone started moving toward the dining room in response to a signal I'd missed. Cherry and I hauled Merry to her feet.

I said to the room in general, "I'll just take some food over to Nick's. I don't know how long moving him will take." I did my best not to cheer that my escape from the big family dinner was succeeding.

Dad scowled. I pushed past him and the kitchen crew to find plastic containers to fill. The combined kitchen smells had nauseated me, but when right under my nose, the aromas of my individual favorites—turkey, cranberries, cornbread dressing (stuffing in other parts of the country), pumpkin pie—did things to my senses that should have been illegal for food. I shoved my way out the door with cries of "Can't you stay?" ringing in my ears.

Nick's place in Montrose was less than four miles away, but I might as well have crossed the border into another country. Whereas West University Place's theme song could also be "Lawyers in Love," being a bedroom community for the upper class, Montrose could be described as eccentric. Its community promotional materials did so, several times. The truth was it was Gay Town that had allowed other marginalized people to move in.

Both neighborhoods, founded shortly after the turn of the twentieth century, had historic houses, but the ones in West U tended to be multistory white brick, like the one where I grew up, or chichi bunga-lows, like Nick's childhood home. Montrose's historical houses were less than half the size of West U's, typically one-story frame houses in "eccentric colors," like the one where Nick now lived.

It sported bubble-gum pink paint with turquoise trim, a fine example of shabby chic, but leaning more towards shabby than chic. The trim on the west side was starting to peel from the summer sun, like every west-facing wall in Texas. Nevertheless, the biscuit-sized front yard sported a For Sale sign pounded into the dirt. A Sold sign attached to it swung proudly in the wind.

Nick threw open the door before I reached the porch. It was déjà vu all over again, seeing this familiar but older six-foot tall, buff-to-the-max guy, genes and skin color muddled between the Latine and European, like many Texans. I could almost hear the admiring sighs of the hormonally pumped high schoolers who used to follow him down the halls.

I flashed back to that winter scout meeting in the synagogue more than a decade ago. Late to the meeting, Nick had flung open the door. Over the leader's scolding about respecting the space, he sobbed, "My dad threw me out." We forgot about the evening's agenda.

He looked no less panicked and wounded now, just not as gangly. A dog stood beside him. A dog whose head was bigger than a watermelon and reached the top of Nick's leg. A dog built like a barrel who pushed Nick aside to thrust that same head out the door and fasten its gaze on me.

I held up my hands. "I come in peace."

"He's a friend, Saint. Friend. Here, JD, shake hands with me so he'll know."

I shook Nick's hand in a solemn ritual. "His name is Saint?"

"I'm rubbish with names. I was going to call him Bernard, after my boyfriend, but Bernie didn't like it." His features twisted. "It's all for the best, considering he dumped me." He looked down at his dog and stroked the soft ears. "Say hi, Saint."

The Saint Bernard wagged his tail and most of his body, trans-forming in a flash from a guard dog to a panting, drooling goof. He walked over to me and looked up expectantly, like I should pet him.

I looked at Nick. "He's your service dog? I've been hearing for twenty years not to pet a working dog. Has the advice changed?"

"You're right. You don't approach a service dog, but if his owner sends him to you, it's okay to interact with him. You can pet him. Luís Montalván, the public face of military service dogs, was the first to teach his dog Tuesday to say hi. It didn't go over well with the trainers, but people loved it. I taught the command to Saint because he met the public as our fire station mascot. The firefighters loved him too. He's served as a greeter and therapist many times."

"He doesn't get confused between guarding you and meeting the public?"

Nick stepped back into the house. "He wouldn't attack anyone, but he would get between me and whatever he saw as a threat. He's still young. Not even 200 pounds."

I wasn't excited about stepping around the young behemoth to enter the house. "Let's not use the word 'attack,' shall we?"

"He doesn't know what it means. Come on inside, both of you."

One wall of the living room was lined with moving boxes, stacked four high. Christmas gift bags clustered on top of the stack. Nick waved a hand at them. "When I ran out of boxes, I put the smaller things in the gift bags."

I made a noise I called sympathetic. "Are you ready to load?"

"Well, no. I haven't made much headway in the bedroom. I keep—" His voice quavered.

I calculated fitting a wall's worth of boxes and bags in a Hyundai Sonata with two men and a Saint Bernard. "Is Saint coming with you?"

"He has to. He's my service dog." Nick's voice added a dash of panic into the quaver. "I've carried dead children out of burning houses. I've treated people with blood welling in their eye sockets. I've taken inventory of crispy critters. But since the accident, I can't manage my own nerves. I get seizures, migraines, panic attacks."

"My business partner almost made it through zoo vet residency when he had a neurodivergent meltdown, not the same, but still tough to deal with. He's better now, but as a cat vet he sees wounded animals. As the assistant justice of the peace, he visits crime scenes. Those he can handle, but everyday life, not so much." I thought about Johnny's coping mechanisms. "Maybe his cats are his service animals. We all have ways of getting through the day or night. None of what you mentioned erases the knowledge and skills you have."

"Don't they?" His voice rose in pitch and volume. "How can I go out on a call when I might collapse or have a seizure?"

Saint lumbered to his feet and trotted toward me. I crab-stepped out of his way. He pulled a leash from a coat hook and brought it to Nick. He leaned against Nick's leg and nudged him.

"You think we should go for a walk, boy? You're right. It would be good for me. You coming, JD?"

I thought I'd better. I even snapped my coat closed against the wind. Fifteen minutes later I unsnapped it because our pace resembled more of a forced march. I let Nick talk, since I was getting short of breath.

CHAPTER 4

By the time we returned to the house, I'd fit some pieces of Nick's life over the last decade together. His community college studies led him to become a firefighter, and he was certified at Firefighter 2 and Emergency Medical Training before he was thirty. Impressive, but not surprising. Nick was smart.

He was on track to become one of the youngest captains when the fire truck he was riding in flipped upside down in a freak accident, trapping the crew for what felt like forever. The rest of the crew walked away with quickly healed minor injuries, but the experience broke Nick's body, brain, and mind. After the accident, he suffered from migraines, seizures, panic attacks, and PTSD.

With such a medical condition, he couldn't go on calls. He held some hope of his brain injury healing over time, but time was taking the long way around. Until then, he had Saint to help him.

His longtime boyfriend Bernie, an older man he met while in college, moved heaven and earth to get Saint for him after the accident. It's not like shelters have fully trained assistance dogs waiting to be adopted.

Nick's station kept him on, with Saint as their mascot, while he did all the admin work, most of the cooking, dispatch, and a good part of the truck washing. He knew they couldn't keep carrying him forever. When Bernie got a job in North Carolina, Nick was relieved to go along and figure out what to do with the rest of his life, now that he couldn't do the one thing he wanted to do.

Nick turned in his notice to the station in November. Bernie broke up with him on December 22 and gave him until the end of the year to move out. Nick thought they'd have a wistful farewell of a holiday season, but instead Bernie went to Galveston to visit friends by himself. He wasn't returning until after New Year's, when he expected Nick gone.

His dog leaned hard against him whenever he got close to breaking down, which was every few minutes, once we returned to the pink house. I offered the food I'd brought, but Nick wasn't interested. Since I hadn't eaten since breakfast, I worked my way through my aunt's cornbread dressing while I talked with Nick.

I expressed breakup sympathies, agreeing with Nick's scurrilous description of Bernie and his ancestry, but guided him toward the issue of moving out. To quote one of the Shakespearean monologues I had to memorize in high school Honors English, "'twere well it were done quickly."

As a sadly single young man, I've helped lots of people move, often after breakups. When you're a lean six-foot-three, people assume you can pick up things. The way it's supposed to go is the mover, also known as me, shows up.

I did.

The mover then asks where the stuff is. No, the friend is never all the way packed, also true in the current case.

All involved load the possessions in the vehicle or vehicles. I hadn't started, because even what I could see wouldn't fit in my car.

I went on to the next step. I asked where the boxes, etc., were going. If it was nearby, we'd just make multiple trips.

Nick's jaw tightened. "I haven't worked that out. I'm not asking Bernie's friends. I thought they were mine too—no."

"I bet your fellow firefighters—"

Nick reached down to pat Saint, who was licking his hand. "I've sponged off them too long, not able to pull my weight. Since I can't have their backs anymore, I was relieved to be leaving."

I thought about Jessa's email and took a chance. "Would your family—?"

Nick swung around with so much force that I stepped back. "My *family*? The mother who left when I was twelve, never to be heard from again? The father who threw me out in the street when I was seventeen? The lying, bullying stepbrother—"

I pulled out my phone and stepped forward, despite his blazing eyes. "I had in mind your stepsister, who sent me an email the other day, asking how to find you."

His fists clenched. "You *told* her? That pest?"

"I did not. I wanted to ask you first. She said there was some kind of family emergency." I scrambled through my phone to show him. "Wait, she sent a follow-up when I said I hadn't seen you in years. And a photo."

JESSA THORNTON

> Okay, thanks. Let me know if you hear from him or if you think of anybody else I can ask. Mama died last month, and Dad's not doing well. He wants to talk to Nick before he passes. Here's our last photo together, from summer vacation. Merry Christmas.

Nick took my phone and studied the photo of the happy-ish family: the frail, older man with dark splotches and lesions on his face; his anxious, exhausted wife, years and pounds heavier, her face also sporting dark spots and scabs, though smaller; two adult children, Brett and Jessa, whom I remembered from high school, not in a good way.

Nick's lips thinned and disappeared as he scrolled up. "Jessa *Thornton*? He adopted them? He threw me away and adopted *them*?" He clutched the phone in a spasm and jerked his arm back to throw it.

"Hey, it's paid for and uninsured!" I blocked his arm.

Breathing hard and furious, he lowered his arm in exaggerated slow motion. Saint whined in his throat as he pulled himself to his feet and planted himself between us.

Nick staggered to the lumpy old couch and sank down, wiggling to move off the dislodged springs, I guessed.

In slo-mo, so as not to startle Saint, I lowered myself beside Nick. After some butt adjustment, I apologized, trying to keep all of us focused. "Sorry. I thought maybe you'd had some contact over the years."

"No. I'll never forget their disgusted, horrified expressions when Dad told me to leave, that I was a disgrace and he never wanted to see me again. No, the fire station was my family. And now my sperm donor wants to talk to me before he dies?" Nick's shoulders shook.

I fiddled with my phone just for something to do with my hands. "Your dad remarried two years after your mother left, right? You weren't happy about that. Or was it the two stepsiblings you didn't like?"

"All of the above. Brett was a year behind us in school. Jessa, a year behind him."

"I remember Brett as a jerk, Jessa as an annoying brat."

"You remember correctly."

"Okay, no fam—other Thornton equivalents. We need another plan."

"I'm sorry for this mess. I saw your text and jumped at the chance to get out of here." Nick dropped his head in his hands. "I could stay at a hostel until my savings run out."

I winced, thinking of my travels in earlier years. "Most hostels hardly give you enough room to breathe. Could Saint go with you? What about your stuff?"

"Storage unit?"

"Do you have one?"

"No." He pressed his eyes first, then his forehead. "Every time I try to plan, I get a migraine. I can feel one coming on."

Saint felt it too. He lumbered to his feet and pulled Nick's hand with a soft mouth. After Nick stood up, Saint led him to the kitchen. I heard the rattle of a medicine bottle and the sound of pouring water. I got busy on my phone with the Black Orchids house chat. I had a temporary solution, but it didn't thrill me.

I also forwarded Jessa's email and photo, because Johnny likes forensic cases to study. As assistant justice of the peace, he gets to decide whether deaths in Alvarez County need more investigation.

Nick staggered back with a granola bar in hand and said, "I'd better lie down for a while. Nothing really helps besides passing out in a dark room."

When my phone pinged, I looked down at it. "Before you go, how's this for a plan? We're not going anywhere today. Tomorrow we'll rent a small trailer. I've already got a trailer hitch, but my car can pull only 1,000 pounds. Question: How does Saint feel about cats?"

"He loves all animals, all people."

"Swell. We'll go to my home in Beauchamp, just south of Austin. I live with my partners in an old mansion on the Historic Register. We've also got an efficiency apartment in the backyard that we can fix up. That would give you time to plan your next chapter." I tried to sound welcoming. Gregg House had felt like a boardinghouse all through the fall, and I had been looking forward to being alone with just the resident people and cats. I mentally kicked myself for that attitude when I lived in a 4,000 square-foot house.

Nick's expression made it clear he wanted to object. He rubbed his forehead again, but he was losing to the migraine. Saint pulled his hand toward the bedroom.

He sighed in surrender. "Thanks. I'm happy to pay rent."

"Nobody's happy to pay rent. Let's give it a couple of weeks and then see how the future looks."

"I appreciate it," he said through clenched teeth. He shut the bedroom door but opened it a minute later and tossed out a pillow and a couple of blankets. "There's food in the pantry."

I took inventory of the kitchen in the fading daylight. Granola bars, gas station burritos wrapped in cellophane, oatmeal. Tap water to drink.

The Christmas feast leftovers won out. I threw them in the microwave. I almost talked myself into going to a convenience store for whatever kind of alcohol they had in the cooler, but I couldn't tell from the pantry and fridge contents what Nick drank. That's my rule; I share what I'm drinking.

I also thought about making an exception for Christmas, but if the store had anything left, it was likely warm beer.

I returned to the couch and discovered that it pulled out into a bed. I sat down with my phone again and sent a confirmation text to my partners that I'd be bringing home new residents. I then sent a text to my sisters, asking if they wanted to do something tonight.

Merry responded before I laid my phone down. "If you're going home tomorrow, would you take me too?"

CHAPTER 5

I called Merry. She felt the same way she did all the time now, just a little worse each day. She had thought she, Cherry, and the grandparents were driving back to their home in Waco the next day. They weren't. Long-time Houston residents, the Grands wanted to spend more time with friends and family.

Merry sobbed, "I understand, but I'd been counting the hours until I could flee, and now I'm stuck in Houston. The Grands and Cherry promised to be back by New Year's Eve, but I just want to get out of this smothering crush of family. If some relative pokes my belly one more time!"

I got the message. I asked if she'd mind driving to Beauchamp with Nick and me and Saint. I'd settle him and the dog, and she and I could drive to Waco in the morning.

She sighed and asked, forlorn, "Not tomorrow night?"

"I doubt we'll leave before noon, what with having to load all Nick's stuff. Then Nick and I will have to unload everything. I'd rather start fresh in the morning on the two-hour drive to Waco. Only Johnny is at Gregg House. He won't be in your face. He never is."

She sighed again. "Right. We can go the next day. I know you're getting older, more tired and everything."

I would have suspected Cherry of master's level manipulation, but

Merry probably thought she was being considerate. I fought the urge to promise her we'd go to Waco tomorrow night. Call it maturity or fear, I've learned not to make rash promises when life is so good at throwing 148-piece-hand-tool kits into the mix.

I asked if she wanted to do anything that evening. No, she was going back to bed. I asked if my own bed was available. No, out-of-town relatives had claimed it. No one had expected me to stay overnight. I looked down at the sofa and sighed. My feet would hang over the end, even if I slept diagonally. I didn't want to think about the springs.

"It's you and me, baby," I muttered as I snagged the blankets and pillow.

Nick slept in the next morning. I didn't. I left a note for him and went out in search of breakfast. I considered the Common Bond Bistro and Bakery but went with Snooze because I wanted a full meal. I recommend the pineapple upside-down pancakes with sides of fluffy eggs and their signature bacon. Between sips of fresh-squeezed juice and bites of pancake, I searched on my phone for a trailer. Hauling boxes would be better than the wild animals I've hauled to help Johnny in his Assistant Animal Control Officer job. The wild hog was the worst. Fortunately he's got a truck now.

The hog would not have fit in any of the minuscule trailers available to me the day after Christmas. Neither would Nick's possessions. I made another call to the West U house and asked my dad if Nick could store some of his stuff in the garage for a while. I didn't want Nick to use his money on a storage unit, if we could avoid it, but my stomach sank like it used to when my younger self asked my father for something wildly unreasonable, like could I borrow the car to take my sisters to their activities.

He expelled the same huff I remembered that boded no good for anybody. "How long?"

"I'm not sure because Nick doesn't have firm plans, but I would think we could get back to Houston within a week or two. I'm taking him home to Beauchamp." I gave Dad a Cliffs Notes version of Nick's recent life and won a grudging consent.

Nick was stumbling about when I returned. I handed him a bag of breakfast sandwiches from Snooze and told him that unless he had any better ideas, we'd be renting the only trailer I could find and storing boxes and bags in my dad's garage until we were down to a single full trailer and trunk. Then we and Merry would get on the road to Beauchamp.

"Merry," he mumbled as he made his way to the kitchen table. He was obviously struggling in the clutches of a migraine aura, the headache's parting gift, and the fuzziness of the drug he took, something powerful. He tore off a small part of the sausage sandwich and handed Saint the larger portion.

While he packed, tying things in sheets and pillowcases, I arranged for the trailer and more boxes. After we loaded the trailer and car, he stayed behind to pack the boxes while I went to Rice Boulevard and unloaded.

I'd hoped to find helpers, but it's a tradition in my family to leave behind the remains of the holiday feast and go out for Mexican food on the day after Christmas. It's called Boxing Day, the Feast Day of St. Stephen, or Synaxis of the Theotokos, none of which had any meaning for my family, but they still celebrated. Between Mexican brunch and the Clearance Sales shopping brigade, I was on my own, except for Cherry, who'd remained behind with her sister. In a feat of extreme generosity, she came out and tossed some gift bags from the car to a corner of the garage.

When I returned to the pink house for what I hoped was the last time, Nick was slumped on the floor in the bedroom by a pile of clothes. Some of them looked like Ren Fair costumes, some Halloween costumes, some matching shirts. Photos and souvenir programs poked out of the jumble.

"I don't need this stuff," he half-sobbed. "But it's Bernie's and my life together, when we were happy, and I can't make myself throw it away."

"You don't have to," I advised. "The storage problem is solved. Throw it in a box or two, label it, and deal with it later."

Saint had another idea. He shuffled to his feet and lumbered over to the pile. He squatted and peed with a powerful sizzling sound. Nick and I both choked on the acrid smell.

Nick's brow cleared. "That's sorted then. I'll get a garbage bag. Poor Saint! It's been hours since I took you outside. I'm sorry, boy. Let me get this stuff into the trash and we'll walk around the block."

That would leave me to load the rest of the boxes. Still, I looked at the dog with new respect. His tongue lolled out, and I swear he was laughing.

CHAPTER 6

Figuring I deserved a break, or at least lunch, I flopped on the couch with one of the granola bars while Nick and Saint took their trip around the block. When we took his things to the Thompson house to store, we definitely had to snarf a plate of holiday cuisine before we hit the road.

By the time we loaded the last boxes, pink clouds tumbled across the sky as the opening act to the standard fabulous Texas sunset. The white bricks of the West U house glowed pink by the time we pulled into the driveway.

As a result of the text I'd sent her before departing the Montrose house while Nick gave it a one-finger salute, Merry was sitting in the breakfast nook with a backpack and my large gift bag at her feet. The blue robe puffed out like a muffin top. A body pillow lay across two chairs beside her.

"We opened the rest of the gifts in your bag," she informed me.

Carrying a plate of Christmas dinner reruns, Cherry joined us from the kitchen proper. "Things from your roommates. I love Johnny's peppermint fudge." She shoved the plate in front of Merry.

"I didn't understand Dianne's gift. She says she'll organize a cuarentena for me?" Merry pushed her plate away and handed me a Christmas card from the gift bag.

I opened it and read Dianne's note. "I've seen Dianne take part in them. One friend or relative visits a new mother every day for forty days and cleans house, prepares food, doing everything to allow the mother to just be with the baby."

Cherry pushed the plate back. "Thank Dianne on behalf of Granny and me, who'd normally be doing all that. Merry, you have to eat something."

"I ate some of Johnny's fudge."

Cherry scowled and looked like she'd weep at the same time, an interesting expression. "Merry, you're eating for two. Possibly sixteen."

"I'm not hungry."

"I am. Nick and I didn't have lunch." I seized a nearby fork.

Merry perked up. "Nick's here? Where?"

"Walking his monstrous canine, in disguise as the biggest service dog you'll ever see. Here, you eat a bite and I'll eat a bite."

"What am I? Six?" With her lower lip jutting out, she looked six.

Cherry snapped, "JD, don't eat her food. She needs it."

I took a dainty bite of the red stuff. "What did you think of Johnny's cranberry mush? You know he's going to ask."

Merry poked an indifferent fork and brought it back with a half inch of red coloring. "It was good. It always is."

"But he keeps changing it. Have another bite so you can tell him how you liked the curry and chocolate chip addition," I urged.

Merry stopped with her fork halfway to her mouth. "Really?"

Cherry snorted and picked up another fork. "Nobody would do that. Okay, you would, JD." She tasted it. "I told you so. It does not have curry and chocolate chips."

"But what is it?" I asked. "He never says because he wants to know if you can taste it."

Merry licked her fork. "Doesn't he usually dump a bottle of bourbon in? I don't think he did this time. It tastes kind of island-y, but I don't know what those spices would be."

Nick and Saint entered the back door at that point. Both twins gasped.

Nick smiled for the first time since I'd seen him. "Hi, this is Saint, my service dog. Shake hands with me. That way he'll know we're friends."

Both women stuck out hesitant hands. They'd had experience with Beauchamp's quasi-police dog who often mixed up her commands.

Saint wagged his tail, knocking the spindly kitchen table chairs awry. He gave Merry's plate a lingering look before turning soulful eyes to her face.

"Can he have some turkey?" she asked Nick.

"Eat it yourself. I'll fix the rest of us—you too, Saint—a plate." I made my way into the kitchen and dished up food for Nick and Saint.

After I plopped both plates in front of Nick, Cherry twisted my arm behind my back and marched me into the living room by the wide front windows.

"Hey, you've taken self-defense classes. Congratulations!"

She hissed in a whisper. "After what happened to my sister? You better believe it. How did you know?"

I lowered my voice to match her volume, even though we could hear Merry in the kitchen laughing with Nick. "Because I've had at least ten female roommates. They all wanted to practice on me. You've got good form, but you could be a tad gentler. Ask Johnny for some pointers."

"The people I'm practicing for don't deserve gentle."

"Your practice partners do. You can let go now. I won't flee or attack you. What's up?"

"Don't you dare drop Merry off in Waco by herself."

"Thank you for that sage advice. Otherwise, I might have pushed my pregnant, not-feeling-good sister out of the car and peeled out. I'll take her to Beauchamp tonight, and tomorrow when we go to Waco, I'll take my laptop and stay with her until somebody returns."

Cherry switched from virago to gawky girl in a flash. "If you have to work, I could come back with you. I just wanted, I wanted ..."

"You wanted to see your friends and have a day off from taking care of your sister, however much you love her. You've been a hero throughout all this." I put an arm around her shoulders in a quick hug.

Tears welled in her eyes, making her eye makeup gooey. "Of course I want to help her, but it's been long and hard, and then there will be a baby.

You can't tell me that will be any easier." Cherry looked out the front windows, but not at the glowing sunset. "I don't understand her. I'd stab myself in the gut with kitchen shears before I'd have my rapist's baby."

I winced at her bald words. "I don't either, but it was her decision. I'll see if she wants to stay in Beauchamp a few days. The cats and Saint might make her happy."

"Make sure she eats!" Cherry finally released my arm.

"Johnny will be cooking. She'll eat, if only to keep from hurting his feelings." I flexed my fingers and shrugged my abused shoulder before putting my arm around her and nudging her back to the kitchen.

"She's probably fed that dog half the plate I fixed for her," Cherry complained in her normal waspish tones.

But Merry looked up and smiled when we re-entered the kitchen. "We were talking about the doll house Nick made for us. JD, remember when Mommy gave us her Madame Alexander dolls from when she was little, and they wouldn't fit in the Barbie houses?"

"And Dad went ballistic over the Madame Alexander accessory prices? Who could forget?" Cherry added as she scanned Merry's plate with a frown.

Its components did look disturbed. I didn't think Saint ate the corn-bread dressing or the cranberries. Maybe a roll.

Merry beamed at Nick. "And you built a dollhouse and furniture for them. When Dad made us clean out our things so he could sell this place, we packed away the house and the dolls to save for our daughters. I can't wait until Jadey's old enough to play with them." Still smiling, Merry patted her belly.

"We did," confirmed Cherry. "The dollhouse looked better than a Barbie mansion when he was done."

Nick's features quivered with pleasure and awe. He looked down and stirred the dressing on his plate. "It makes me feel good that you kept something I made. JD helped, too. It was a team effort."

That's not how I remembered it, but I'd take the shout-out. "Nick was always better at it than me."

"True," agreed Cherry.

I shot her a brotherly glare. Hearing a car in the driveway, I jumped to my feet. "We should get going. Cherry, will anyone mind if we take some of the feast home?" All I'd had to eat since the granola bar were mini-bites from Merry's plate.

"It's my house too, and I say yes. I mean, no, they won't mind. Because I won't tell them." She even got to her feet and helped, not the treatment I've come to expect from Charity Adrienne Thompson. I've been laughing at her name since she was five and hogging the kindergarten snacks.

By the time my grandparents, my father, and Mallory came in the back door, Nick had scooped up Merry's backpack, bag, and body pillow. I held plastic grocery sacks full of food in front of me like Birnam Wood. I caught a glimpse of Mallory, recently the object of my desire ... affection ... whatever. Seeing her next to my father—no, I still couldn't process that without nausea.

We couldn't get out the door as fast as I wanted. Everyone had to greet Nick. Saint blocked the doorway too, wagging his tail like a bridge troll demanding toll. I surreptitiously showed him a piece of turkey and then threw it over everyone's heads into the backyard. He didn't take off like lightning, but he didn't have to. He stood as wide as the door. People fell back to let him pass, faster than his usual amble, close to a trot.

I blustered after him with my load, echoing insincerely the regrets of Mallory and the grandparents that we hadn't had any time to talk.

When we made it to the highway, all the occupants sighed in relief. Maybe Saint's wasn't relief, but he did sigh as every part of him sank down into the blanket Nick had spread out for him on the right side of the backseat behind Merry. We'd learned earlier to put down his seat back for him to stretch out with his back end in the trunk. I turned on my playlist, the one I call "Calm the @#$@!! Down," full of soothing ballads. No one objected. The playlist was having its usual soporific effect.

I looked in the mirror back at Nick. He was ruffling the fur on Saint's head. Since Nick hadn't said anything, I assumed he was okay riding in a car after his accident, though it occurred in a fire truck. Because PTSD isn't predictable, I mentally planned a couple of stops along the way, more if he or Saint indicated. I glanced at Merry. I hadn't known many pregnant women, but they all demanded near and constant access to a bathroom.

Merry's cheeks shone with tears. She made little sniffling sounds I wouldn't have noticed over the music if I hadn't been looking at her.

"JD?" she whispered in a high-pitched chirp, like a four-year-old. "I'm sorry, JD. I peed on your car seat. I didn't know I had to go. I'm sorry. Really sorry."

"That's okay, Sissy," I said, appalled but not wanting to show her. She was upset enough for both of us. I could always cut the seat out or buy a new car.

Nick leaned forward to put his right hand on her shoulder. Saint moved forward and tried to stick his head over the opposite side of her seat. "I'm sure JD understands, Merry. JD, pull over and let me confirm what I suspect, that her water's broken."

Horrified, she looked back as far as she could twist, confined by the seatbelt and pregnancy. "That can't be true. I'm nowhere near due. Also, could Saint stop drooling in my hair?"

CHAPTER 7

There's never a gas station, gift store, or restaurant along the highway when you need one. Saint continued panting, just because he was a dog, no particular reason. Nick scooted Saint further back to avoid his drooling on Merry.

Nick murmured to Merry in a soft voice. I couldn't make out the words. I'm not sure she could either. Her quiet sobbing sounded like a substitute for breathing.

My mouth was dry and my tongue thick. I swallowed over and over, faster the longer we traveled. After only a month or two—or was it minutes?—I spotted sets of blinding commercial lights. I whooshed a relieved sigh and pulled into a parking lot.

"I am not giving birth in the parking lot of Buc-ees," screamed Merry.

I eased the car in the lot and parked on the side of the building. I didn't want people to see us as they walked to the entrance from their cars. "They say you can find anything at a Buc-ees. Maybe a doctor?"

"Looks more like a Stuckey's," said Nick. "And you're probably a ways from giving birth, Merry."

"It's not a chain store at all," I announced after scanning the signs and building. "It's that locally owned pecan and gift store. That's better, right? I've often stopped here to pick up a pecan pie to take to Houston. They'll probably give you one."

"I hate you both! You're idiots." Merry raised her volume to a painful level. It dropped back down to little girl territory as she whimpered to Nick, now out of the car and opening the front passenger door, "You're not going to *look* at me down there, are you?"

Nick's voice was smooth as butter at a summer picnic. "I don't need to do that, and I wouldn't do anything without your consent. I'm a trained and certified firefighter and Emergency Medical Technician, but I know it's hard to think of me as anything but your brother's childhood friend. I would like to look at the fluid. Can I help you get out of the car for a minute and put one of Saint's blankets down? JD, you search for the nearest hospital."

"We need that?" I fumbled, trying to connect my phone's GPS with the car's dashboard. That simple task eluded me.

"Yes. No choice about it." He handed me his phone, shining bright, and a blanket before getting out of the car and opening the passenger door. Saint waddled after him. "Turn sideways and put your arms around me, Merry. I'll lift you up, just for a second. JD, shine the light on the seat." For all Nick's talk about being weak, he lifted her up gracefully and sniffed. "Good news, Merry. You didn't pee on the seat. Your water broke. Even better news: you'll have your baby in your arms within twenty-four hours. JD, put the blanket on the seat."

I settled the folded blanket, and Nick returned Merry to her seat.

After several more taps, my electronics sprang to life. I asked, "Should we go back to Houston, Nick? Brampton is less than fifteen minutes away, and it's associated with a university."

"Saint, say hi to Merry. JD, let's go to Brampton. It's further to go back. I'm not sure we'd get any help if we did."

"It's too soon," Merry whimpered. Saint shoved Nick aside and laid his head in her lap. She stroked his ears.

"Babies have a way of ignoring calendars. The hospital will take good care of you both. They work miracles nowadays. Merry, you ought to call your doctor, but let's head to Brampton rather than hang out here." Nick's soothing voice calmed me down too.

It was more like ten minutes (at least three songs, whose gentle crooning now annoyed me) until we arrived at the emergency room. I kept putting my foot on the brake when I noticed the speedometer. Ninety percent of my panicking, bouncing brain cells screamed at me to hurry. The other ten percent knew that wrecking the car wouldn't help anyone. I was so far out of my wheelhouse here, conscious of the uselessness of any skillset I could claim. I hadn't even earned the scout badge for delivering babies.

When we pulled into the ER drop-off, orderlies sprang for our car with a wheelchair. I went with Merry, leaving the car for Nick to park.

"Did you reach your doctor?" I whispered.

She turned a tear-stained face to me. "She's not on call, and her substitute said to go to the nearest hospital."

"Nice to know we've followed orders."

The hospital was sleek and new, all metal and glass, with corners sharp enough to cut. The waiting room overflowed with people having a very bad day, like most ERs on a holiday. It smelled like the usual cleaning products, but they were losing the battle with unwashed, sick people and vending machine food.

The intake desk still sported its tinsel, now sagging and bedraggled. The attendant swiped a thermometer across my sister's forehead. She frowned at the instrument and asked standard questions. Merry gasped out her information in a tiny voice with odd pauses when she hunched over her belly. For some reason, the nurse wanted to know the dates of her last period. Any idiot could see that was a long time ago.

I asked if I could finish checking her in while they took her back to be seen. "Do you mind leaving your purse with me, Merry? I need to get your insurance card."

She shook her head and handed me a little clutch bag. "I was trying to find it in the car, but it was too dark."

"I'm not sure we can see her," said the intake nurse, red-eyed, shoulders sagging. "Let me check."

"What?" squeaked Merry. "What am I supposed to do?"

I pulled out my phone and called Nick. "Can you come in? We need a native speaker of medical-ese."

The front doors flew open to admit Nick and Saint just as the nurse came back, drooping even more.

She raised her voice and pointed at Saint. "You can't bring that dog in here."

"I can. He's my service dog, and I'm in the allowable areas," Nick assured her.

The waiting room patients seemed to feel Saint was the most exciting thing that had happened since the event that brought them to the hospital. Adults turned to look and smile through their pain, and children raised cries of "Doggy!"

I put a hand on Merry's shoulder and addressed the intake worker. "And I'm his lawyer, here to make sure you treat him in accordance with the ADA. Let's skip the dog for the moment." I was going to have to refresh myself on those laws. "Can you take my sister back now, please? Nick's an EMT. He can talk to you about her condition."

The nurse took on an anguished expression. "I'm sorry, Ms. Thompson. We can't treat you. If you go home and lie down, the contractions might stop."

"I'm giving birth!" she exclaimed. Her face twisted in pain. "I think."

"She obviously needs medical attention," I declared. "We brought her here on the advice of our EMT. He thought a hospital was better than delivering the baby in the car."

"Ms. Thompson, based on the information you gave us, the law won't let us interfere." Her face looked as pained as Merry's. She seemed to have less agency than a big box store greeter. "I wish we could help."

"Her water broke," said Nick. "My training taught me to take the patient to the hospital immediately."

"Calculating from the date of her last period—"

"Calculating!" I exploded. "We don't have to calculate. We know the exact date of conception. I can show you the police report."

Nick took in a sharp breath. "Police report!"

Merry settled in to cry in earnest.

I put a hand on each of her shoulders and pressed my cheek against her tangled, blonde hair. "It's grim, Nick. Merry, I'm going to wheel you over by the treatment doors. I need to be a lawyer for a minute."

She clutched my arm. "JD, don't leave me!"

"You don't want to see my full combat mode, Sissy." I turned the chair and pushed it toward the swinging doors.

Nick twitched Saint's leash. "Saint will stay right with you, Merry, and I'll stand between you and JD, available to either one of you if you need me." He let out the leash almost to its full length. He met my eyes. "I have to have the leash in my hand at all times."

Merry shifted in her seat. "I think I should go to the bathroom first."

I let her take care of that issue. I turned my eyes back to the nurse and silently called on generations of my family lawyers for a voice as arctic as the weather. "Please explain to me in very short sentences why you will not treat a pregnant woman in distress so that I can explain to her father, Attorney Jay Thompson; her grandfather, former U.S. Attorney Jim Thompson; her cousin Judge James Thompson; her uncles, aunts, and cousins who are attorneys; and the rest of the family who loves her. I seem to recall a federal law about providing stabilizing care for patients in extremis."

The nurse's face froze into something inhuman, at least inhumane. "We can't provide care that might be construed as an abortion under Texas law."

"Merry doesn't want an abortion. Her family wants to save both Merry and her child. Why can't you help with that?"

"Sir, we no longer have a neonatal unit. We're closing all maternity services next year. They're too risky under current law."

Nick had been inching forward. "Could you at least examine her? We need to know what we're dealing with."

"And refer us to some place that can help her?" I added.

"No. No. Here's a brochure. You'll have to let nature take its course." With her last drop of compassion, she threw Merry a sorrowful glance before backing away and turning toward the door behind the desk, the escape hatch.

I called after her, "At least give me a legal contact for this place."

A gruff voice right behind me said, "You can call the hospital during working hours tomorrow."

I felt a hand on my arm and looked back into the eyes of a burly security officer. Another one approached Nick who held his hands up and backed toward Merry and Saint, sitting beside her with his head in her lap.

"You can't have that dog in a hospital!" yelled the second officer. Though he was smaller than the guy behind me gripping my arm, he looked leaner and meaner.

Saint stood to attention, awaiting a command. Merry kept her fingers tangled in his rough fur.

"He's a service dog, as it says on his vest. Federal law allows him in certain areas of the hospital, including this one." My sigh turned into an "Ouch" as the security officer did something to my elbow. "We're leaving, we're leaving. All of us. If you'll turn me loose, I'll wheel my sister to the door, and Nick will lead his dog."

My goon freed my arm, but not without an extra twist. I'd already given myself away with my "ouch," but I refused to rub the arm. It felt weak after his grip. Nick reeled in the leash and put Saint between him and everyone else. I smiled at Merry and patted her shoulder as I wheeled her to the exit. I had no idea what to do next.

CHAPTER 8

Nick turned to me at the doorway. "I've still got the keys. All of you wait here, and I'll drive the car up to the door. You too, Saint. Stay." He handed me the leash and ruffled the dog's fur as the huge canine behind plunked down on the floor.

"You can't stand in front of the door," growled the first security officer.

I smiled and wedged Merry's chair over a few inches, away from the center of the doorway. "Just for a minute, until he brings the car around. I don't mind moving, but nobody but Nick can move Saint." Hearing his name, Saint looked up at me and panted.

"That dog shouldn't be in here."

I sighed. "The Americans with Disabilities Act says otherwise."

Nick swung the car in front of the door before anyone could point out that the disabled person wasn't in the room. I moved forward to let the automatic doors open, but Nick waved me back. "Wait inside until I get the car set up for Merry. It's too cold for her to be outside."

Being a firefighter must have made him quick, a lot quicker than he had been about packing. Before Security could blow up at us, he had blankets and pillows in the back seat. "We'll put Saint in the front seat. Merry, let's put you in the back, sideways, with your feet across the seat and a pillow behind your back."

Icicle stilettos hit my face when I stepped into the cold wind.

"Can I have a blanket over me too?" Merry shifted herself to her feet and clutched her coat closer. It didn't cover her bump at all. Wishing for gloves, I kept my hands on the wheelchair until she was completely inside the car.

Nick frowned into the trunk area. "I'm running out of blankets—"

"Get her robe. It's sticking out of one of the gift bags," I advised.

"Good thinking."

I crossed to the opposite side of the car to get it started and warm us all up. Nick covered Merry up to her chin in blue velour and came around to the passenger side to load Saint into the front seat beside me.

I eyed the dog dubiously as Nick shoved him.

"Saint," panted Nick. "Come on, boy. Up!"

Gravity seemed to be working twice as hard on Saint, but he did make it up onto the seat and grinned in triumph. Glancing down at his massive paws and claws, I was glad Merry's first blanket still covered the seat. Saint didn't seem to mind the dampness.

I warmed my hands in my armpits while the car's heater blasted, not much warmer than its air conditioning. "Any ideas, Mr. EMT? Should we head back to Houston? We're a little over halfway to Beauchamp."

"Unless you know of a place that will admit her, I'd say push on. I've seen this attitude in hospitals a lot recently, and I've delivered more babies in the last year than in my whole career. It's one kind of call the station would send me on, at least as an assistant."

"Good to have an experienced EMT on board. Right, Merry?"

"I'm great with normal births," Nick's flat voice emphasized the contrast with Merry's condition. He contorted himself into the backseat and lifted Merry's feet onto his lap. "Mostly that's about catching the baby and not dropping it."

"I'll call my partner. He's in the medical field."

"Your partner is a vet," Merry sobbed.

"And he's delivered everything from kittens to calves. Maybe horses too. More importantly, he knows medical people. His grandmother's a nurse. They should have some advice for us."

Johnny picked up on the first ring. I explained the situation. He asked me to repeat it.

"I'm having trouble understanding a hospital refusing treatment," he said after my third attempt.

"We all do," I responded. "You can ask Dianne or your grandmother about it later. They have opinions. But the hospital threw us out, and now we need to find a way to take care of Merry and her child."

"I'm in Austin having dinner with my grandmother and sister," he replied. "I'll call my grandmother over. By the way, were the parents in that photo you sent me diagnosed with the same thing? They both look near death."

"Jessa didn't say, just that her mother died recently. I don't know. I doubt if Nick does either."

"What?" thundered Nick from the backseat.

"Your stepmother's and father's illnesses. I sent Johnny the photo from Jessa. He's assistant justice of the peace for Alvarez County, and he's always looking for cases to study in case something similar comes his way."

"He can study away. DKDC." In case we didn't know, Nick added, "Don't know, don't care."

His phone rang. He answered with a snarl.

I didn't hear a response from Johnny, but Mrs. Ly's voice boiled with fury as she fired medical questions at me. I answered what I could. "Out of my wheelhouse. Hold on. Here's Merry and—"

Merry moaned.

Nick whispered into his phone in a voice he didn't mean to be heard. Saint's panting and Merry's groans almost covered it up. "I didn't steal Saint. You gave him to me. You said he was mine. I've cared for him for two years."

I held my phone over my shoulder. "Nick, trade phones with me and talk to the medical team I've assembled. A vet and a nurse, but they're better assistants than a lawyer."

Nick's face was tight and furious as he thrust his phone out. "It's my ex, Bernie. He says I stole Saint." He accepted my device.

A lawyer's work is never done. Someone's always being a jerk or a criminal. "Hey, Bernie. I'm Nick's attorney. He's dealing with a medical emergency right now. You can submit your request to JD Thompson, Attorney at Law, in Beauchamp, Texas. Nick and I will review it while we're assembling his record of two years of care and supplies, which I feel confident will outweigh any investment you made. Be sure to forward the contract between you and Nick. Also, you might consider whether you want the publicity of ripping a young hero's support dog away from him."

"Especially the fire station spokesman whose picture's been in the paper twice since Thanksgiving and featured three times in the Houston Firefighter's calendar," shouted Nick from the backseat. "And there is no freaking contract."

As soon as he started speaking, I held the phone in his direction. "You really want to come for the Fire Department's Mr. November, Bernie? Gotta go. Talk to you soon."

CHAPTER 9

"Mr. August," Nick corrected me. "I was Mr. November in last year's calendar."

Merry asked, "Can I buy some of your calendars? My sister and my friends would like them, and I didn't get them much for Christmas."

"My grandmother would like one too," I said.

"Really?" she squeaked and then groaned.

Nick and I exchanged phones, and he reached around into the passenger seat to hug as much of Saint as he could. He pressed his head hard into the back of the seat.

"Migraine?" I asked.

He sat up straight and then slumped in his seat. "Just misery. I used to think that Bernie must love me because he went through hell to get me a trained service dog. I think he expected Saint to fix me, make me normal again, and neither Saint nor anybody else can do that. Saint makes it possible for me to get up every day and go on, but pre-accident me is gone for good."

"Too bad he wasn't willing to see how you could be post-accident."

Nick snorted. "You're not going to tell me about the Japanese repairing pottery with gold, are you?"

"Kinsugi? Nah, I wouldn't do that. Did Mrs. Ly have any advice? I'll get on the road if you tell me which way we're going."

Nick rubbed his forehead and called up his healer persona. "She said there's no point in driving to hospitals when we don't know if they'll admit Merry. I told her I didn't think Merry was well established in labor—I'm sorry, Merry. I know bad labor hurts just like good labor. She said she'll keep calling hospitals, but she doesn't expect to find one. If not, she'll meet us in Beauchamp, and we can sit with Merry and see if her labor progresses to the point we can convince a hospital to take her. In that case, we'll call an ambulance to take her to the nearest hospital. How far away is that?"

"We've always called San Mateo, eighteen miles away, going north toward Austin on I-35, which everyone tries not to do."

"San Mateo?" He sounded anxious.

That was an odd reaction for a sleepy college town. I decided it didn't matter at the moment. Getting help for Merry took precedence. "That's the nearest. A former client is an administrator there.* Maybe he can help us."

Nick's eyes closed and his features sagged. Merry stiffened and cried out, kicking him in the process. He patted her leg. "You're doing great. Have you ever meditated?"

"Every blasted day, because my therapist said to."

"Me too, for the same reason. Let's see if some of the breathing techniques will help get you through this."

I drove to Beauchamp with ABBA and other groups moaning soothing melodies. I tried to pretend I was fifteen and driving my mother and little sisters to see Christmas lights. It didn't work, not with Saint panting beside me and Nick and Merry panting and counting breaths in the backseat.

We had the pitch-black night to ourselves. Most people were still living their Christmassy life. Those who weren't needed to get up for work in the morning. I traveled a good part of the way with my bright lights on, mostly swallowed by the night.

Relief flooded me like a drug when I pulled into the Gregg House

---

* We met Vidal Abreu in *Hallow: A Fractured Family Tale*, Book 5.

parking area in the back. That made no sense, because we'd found only stopgap care for Merry. Still, it was home, more home than the white brick house in West University these days.

Its automatic lights flared as we made our way up the clinic ramp to spare Merry the back porch steps. She could walk (with stops) but sagged against Nick and me. Nick showed me how to support her without strain. Saint stayed close to Nick, giving him support too. Johnny met us at the top of the ramp with his grandmother's rolling walker. Merry sank gratefully into the seat, and we surrounded her, even Saint, because the walker isn't supposed to be used as a wheelchair, as Johnny reminded us.

I pulled Merry's robe around her to keep it off the floor. Always Captain Obvious, I said, "I have the feeling we're going to be using many things off label tonight."

Nick guided Saint to walk in front of us. "It's like the scripture you hear in church this time of year, about the wise men going home by another way. Kind of my motto on the job too: Do everything like you're taught until you can't. Then think of a new way."

My mental blender was whirring on the highest anxiety setting, but I still managed to introduce Johnny to Nick and Saint. If Nick had showed up in the University of Texas dorm all those years ago, life would have been different for all three of us. It was weird to have two possible life paths in the same room.

Johnny and his grandmother had converted the gracious living area to a parody of a medical setting. The heavy, solemn antiques seemed offended at being shoved aside to make room for a hospital bed, unused since Johnny's grandfather's last illness. Adjusted to an angle for Merry to sit, the bed faced the TV, revealed from its hiding place behind the silk tapestry. A portable oxygen tank stood nearby. An end table at the foot of the bed held a tray of tools I hoped I didn't need to know about.

Mrs. Ly, a matriarchal martinet, normally scares me to death. Tonight she was all compassion as she invited Merry and me to sit down. "JD, I had John Ky print a consent form for Merry to sign, the same one I use for all my informal patients. My grandson the lawyer drew it up for me." She spoke with aplomb, but there's no repressing a grandmother's pride.

I took the page she held out and scanned it. "This looks like a standard consent-to-treat form. Merry, it says you know Mrs. Ly isn't a doctor, that she's acting under the Good Samaritan laws to render what aid she can, and you hold her harmless from any results."

"I haven't forgotten how to read." Merry sounded cross. She snatched the page and proved she could read it, though she had to stop once to breathe through a contraction. She turned pathetic eyes toward Mrs. Ly. "What are my choices?"

"You mean do nothing? I don't advise it. The hospital wouldn't admit you because you have a fever and your child is on the edge of viability, and it's less legal trouble for them if you give birth elsewhere." Mrs. Ly patted her hand with a bleak expression. "In Vietnam, we had to make do with whatever we had under limitations we couldn't change. I would never willingly practice under such conditions again, and I'm sorry I lived to see it."

"But my baby could die," Merry whispered.

CHAPTER 10

"Yes. Your baby could die. You could also, but neither is the hospital's worry if you're not in their care."

Merry turned pleading eyes toward me. I tried to encourage her with a smile. "I, for one, am grateful to have such a versatile nurse with my sister. Could we get her airlifted to another state?"

"There are volunteers who do that, but it's not like a rideshare. It would take some time, at least hours to arrange." Mrs. Ly's voice held the patience of medical people who have explained things over and over many, many times.

I frowned. "And in the meantime—"

"What would the hospital do, if they did admit me?" asked Merry in a thin voice.

"Give you antibiotics and monitor your and the baby's vital signs. Urine testing and bloodwork."

"What are you going to do?" Merry struggled to sound like an adult as her hands pushed her legs together.

"Give you antibiotics and monitor your and the baby's vital signs. Sadly, I can't do the bloodwork, though I can do simple urine testing."

Johnny entered our space with an incubator I'd seen him use with his cats. He set it on the coffee table, shoved against the wall under the TV. "I can do some bloodwork. Let me know what you need."

"Why do you have antibiotics and monitors at the ready?" I asked.

She gave me a matriarchal death glare. "When I was the nurse for the Beauchamp school district, several times I delivered babies for girls who came to my office with a stomachache. After the first one, I swore I'd never be unprepared again. Lately it seems my skills and equipment are required again. I have a granddaughter in Texas."

Johnny gave the incubator a last wipe. "She promised to move, Grandmother."

Mrs. Ly turned her laser gaze on her grandson. "Meanwhile, I'm prepared. Merry, what do you want to do?"

Merry picked up the pen and propped the page on the rolling walker arm. That gave her just enough room to sign her full name, slowly, as though she'd just learned how. "Please save my baby."

"My goal is to save you both. Let's get you on the bed so I can examine you.

Merry shot me a panicked look, but she relaxed into Mrs. Ly's firm grasp as the nurse helped her into the bed. Mrs. Ly ordered Johnny and me to set up several tri-fold Vietnamese silk screens for privacy.

Johnny and I went back down the hall to the kitchen-dining area. He stirred the contents of the warming dishes. "I prepared dinner, not knowing if you would have eaten, just leftovers to wrap in tortillas."

"It's been a while," I admitted.

Nick was already at the dining room table. "Always eat when it's offered. You never know how long you're going to be on duty."

"Would your dog like to explore the backyard?" Johnny asked Nick as we headed to the kitchen in the back of the house. "We have an acre of land, plenty of room for him to roam. The fence is sturdy, and I doubt he can jump it."

Nick hesitated. "I'll go out with him for a few minutes, and if he wants to stay out longer, he can. He doesn't get to play by himself much, especially in the cold."

While I searched the freezer for the meat Dianne and I keep prepared for Johnny's vegetarian meals, Johnny took a seat at the table and said, "As a rough-coat Saint Bernard, he's especially suited for cold climates, like the Swiss Alps where the breed originated. I have a client who has llamas. They're from cold regions also. She lets them stay inside her air-conditioned house in the summer."

Nick held the door open for Saint and held up a tennis ball. "I don't want to be outside in the heat any more than he does, so it works fine for us. We go out in the middle of the night and early morning. I'm still acclimated to different hours than the rest of the world from all my shift work. Saint, want to chase the ball? I'll bring in the stuff from the car too."

After the door shut behind them, Johnny asked, "What kind of shift work did he do?"

I skipped the tortilla and crowned my vegetable mélange with bacon instead. "Firefighter and EMT." I gave Johnny a run-down of Nick's history. "I heard from his stepsister the day of our open house, but he's not interested in a reunion. Can't imagine I would be either."

Before eating, I fiddled with my phone, adding family to my friends' text chat for the sake of updating everybody at once on Merry's condition.

"I wouldn't be either. I've always been grateful for my parents' care of their neurodivergent son. Sure, they sent me to college at age sixteen, but I was happy to go. It was easier than high school." Johnny pulled up the photo from Jessa. "That photo you sent me is Nick's family? I'd recommend that his father have a full workup immediately, especially for heavy metals."

"You tell him so then." Nick banged the door shut as he re-entered the house. "Why are you so fascinated with my so-called family?"

I said, "Some people would play video games in their downtime. Johnny does forensic research."

Recognizing a lame joke, the corners of Johnny's mouth gave a dutiful twitch. "As the assistant justice of the peace, I decide whether deaths in the county need further investigation. I study so I can recognize symptoms that would indicate something besides natural causes, like those dark spots on Mr. and Mrs. Thornton's faces. The way they're hunched over might indicate digestive issues or just pain in general."

"Or they could be old." Nick took a plate and a tortilla and surveyed his choices.

"True, and that perception contributes to the low autopsy rate for the elderly. At age fifty-five, a corpse's chance of being autopsied drops to ten percent and to less than two percent by age seventy-five."

I scraped up a forkful of bacon-flavored veggies. "I'd call it close to zero in Alvarez County where the sheriff never wants the expense of an autopsy. Remember that case last summer, when he said the corpse with two bullets was a suicide?"

Johnny continued squinting at my phone. "That's technically possible, but it happens in only 3% of the cases—and not in the one you're referring to."

"It's a laugh a minute around here, isn't it?" Nick made his own soft taco, some of everything and a bucket of salsa.

"Just you wait," I replied.

Mrs. Ly clumped down the hall into the kitchen. "Johnny, Nick, may I count on you as my assistants? I want to monitor Merry's vital signs closely. I'm sure you know how to measure temperature, oxygen saturation, blood pressure, and so on."

They nodded in agreement. She gave the blood pressure duties to Nick, the one most accustomed to taking that measurement on humans. Johnny can wrap a miniature sleeve around a cat patient's tail, but that wouldn't be useful here.

Before I could skip away, happy to be free of any duties, Mrs. Ly continued, "Merry would like you to sit with her, JD. Her labor hasn't been productive, but the contractions are getting stronger and more regular. If that continues, and her cervix dilates, we'll call the ambulance to take her to San Mateo."

As I scooped up the last bite on my plate, I said, "I was thinking of calling a former client who's an administrator there."

Her smile twisted into a sour grimace. "It can't hurt. Time was we'd call a doctor, but we know who runs the medical show now."

CHAPTER 11

I'll never forget that night. I've tried. The combination of terror and boredom still haunts my dreams in painfully etched detail. I don't suppose my sister remembers it any more fondly.

Merry wanted me by her side, and I held her hand. She crushed mine during contractions before I learned how to turn it.

On the big screen TV, I set up majestic landscapes floating by to the rich accompaniment of Brahms, because Merry couldn't concentrate on a show or stand the default Christmas music provided by the landscape program.

Every fifteen minutes Mrs. Ly called for Johnny and Nick, seated on Merry's left and right, to check vital signs: temperature, blood pressure, heart rate, oxygen saturation, pulse, and others I've forgotten. They'd call out numbers that Mrs. Ly, seated at Merry's feet, recorded in a small black notebook. A machine strapped to Merry's belly monitored the baby's heartbeat. I could see why Mrs. Ly acquired all this equipment if girls regularly waddled into her nurse's office thinking they'd been poisoned by the school cafeteria mystery meat.

I looked from one face to another, trying to read their responses. Were the numbers the same or different? What did they mean? Were things getting better or worse? I couldn't tell, and I told myself the lack of reaction was intended to avoid panicking the patient. I panicked anyway.

The hours crawled by.

One crazy memory that sticks out is me walking Merry to the restroom to collect a urine specimen. She leaned hard against me and into Mrs. Ly's rolling walker. Because I wanted to walk in an even beat to give Merry the smoothest possible support on this epic journey, I went over a song, as I thought, in my mind. When she asked me what I was humming, I laughed.

"It's … 'Why Did It Have to Be Me?' Good old ABBA song."

Merry laughed so hard that I eased an arm around her waist to keep her steady. Eventually she managed to speak between snorts. "Never heard it, but it's my theme song."

Merry fell into my pace, an easier gait than her lurching and jerking. By the second chorus, she was belting out "Why did it have to be me?" louder than me. I promised to write suitable words for the verses.

The other distraction that sticks out came from Saint. He enjoyed the backyard, but when his bark changed to something urgent, Nick went to check on him (after taking more measurements).

He showed up some feet back from Merry's bed with something in each hand and a bemused expression on his face. "Saint found two kittens in the backyard. They're pretty cold."

Johnny stood up. "What have you got them wrapped in?"

"Tortillas from your warming pan." Nick held them up for us to see, literal kitten burritos.

Merry managed a soggy smile.

Saint danced by the back door, and Nick went back outside with him (after washing up and taking more measurements). They soon charged back into the house with three more kittens.

"We're out of tortillas," Nick proclaimed.

Because the incubator was for Merry's baby, Johnny dragged a big sheepskin bed with a pet heating pad into the gallery-hall from the clinic. He put the kittens in it where he could see them from Merry's bedside. Saint lay across the whole bed. He snuffled each baby in turn and nuzzled them to his side.

Nick laughed as he returned to Merry's bedside. "We had a stray cat and her kittens at the station last summer. Saint spent more time with them than the mom cat did.

After another set of measurements, Johnny, Nick, and Saint went outside to search for signs of a mother cat. Gregg House is a favorite dumping ground for unwanted litters, with and without mothers.

"Fifteen minutes," Mrs. Ly called after them.

With every minute, my anxiety increased as I dreaded the prospect of operating all the monitoring equipment.

After Nick, Saint, and Johnny went outside together, Merry turned her head toward me. She started to say something, but her eyes widened as a contraction seized her.

I looked around in a panic and repeated the counts I'd heard Nick make.

When it passed, she closed her eyes and whispered, "JD, I changed my mind. I can't do this."

Why did I end up as her support team, of all my family? The only one more unqualified was my father. With the men outside chasing kittens, Mrs. Ly reading her infernal machinery, Dianne in Dallas, Cherry and Grandmother in Houston, Merry had only me.

I remembered one of Dianne's pithy sayings, "JD, if you're the only one left, you're the best one for the job." She was talking about stripping and refinishing the floor, but the principle still applied.

I put an arm around Merry's head and let my hand rest on her opposite shoulder in an awkward hug. "Of course you're over-whelmed. It's true you can't get out of this event. The good news is you don't have to do it all now, and you don't have to do it alone. I'll be right beside you, and all you have to do this minute is take a breath."

She did, but it sounded like a sob.

"That's great. Now another breath."

This one was even more jagged.

"And that's all you have to do, the next breath, until the situation changes. I'm here, and Mrs. Ly is here, and Nick and Johnny will be back in a few minutes. Pretty soon Grandmother and Cherry will be here. They sent a text. And all you need to do is take the next breath."

She made little movements that would have been thrashing if she didn't have the equivalent of a prize-winning pumpkin strapped on her front side.

The breathing continued through the Brahms repertoire—the Piano Quintet after the String Sextets.

Johnny brought in the mother cat, injured, and headed for his clinic. Mrs. Ly promoted me to taking measurements while Merry dozed in and out of consciousness. We were back to boredom.

Then Mrs. Ly said, "It's time for the call, JD."

I dropped my phone.

CHAPTER 12

I scrambled on the floor for it and gave thanks that it was still intact. I fumbled the keys.

"Nine-one-one," Mrs. Ly said helpfully.

The dispatcher answered at that point and asked me questions I knew the answers to. Police or medical emergency. My address. Finally, the reason for my call.

My voice broke into the tenor range, at least half an octave higher than my usual bass-baritone. "My little sister—she's having a baby, but it's too soon. I think she's in trouble. Her water broke. I don't know—can you get here right away?" I held my phone out for Mrs. Ly to give them the expert version, but she shook her head. The dispatcher promised someone would be there soon.

"You did fine." She sighed. "A young panicky man is more convincing than an old nurse."

"Is she going to be all right? Is the baby?" I wished my voice weren't wobbling.

She looked up into my eyes. "I'm doing everything I can, trying to anticipate rather than wait until it's irreversibly bad, but I can't promise anything. Call your hospital administrator client."

I did, pretending I didn't know it was near midnight. Vidal promised to go to the hospital to be available for questions or blame, as the case might be. I mumbled something like "thanks" as I disconnected the call.

Mrs. Ly was putting away the last of her instruments when the ambulance folk pounded on the front door. They and Mrs. Ly threw around medical terms while I held Merry's hand and whispered that she'd be safe in a hospital soon.

As the medics shifted her on to a stretcher, I asked, "Can Mrs. Ly and I ride with you?"

"One of you can ride." The EMT didn't look at me but kept his eyes on Merry as he strapped her to the stretcher.

I found myself blinking tears. I was the most useless person in the room. I touched Merry's head, the only thing I could easily reach without interfering. "Merry, Mrs. Ly will ride with you. I'm following in my car. I won't leave your side after we get to the hospital. Where's your phone?"

Mrs. Ly handed me Merry's backpack, slung across her own suitcase.

"Saint and I will stay with JD," Nick announced.

He and Johnny carted the kittens to the clinic, since their substitute mother was leaving. I made a face call to Merry's phone and dug in her bag to answer it.

Mrs. Ly took it from me. "I'll prop it up for her when we're settled in the ambulance."

"Hear that, Merry? I'll be on the phone with you the whole way." I caught a glimpse of a smile. I think.

I stood outside, shivering, and sent a text blast to family and friends while the ambulance sped away.

Nick met me at the front door. "Go pack an overnight bag. I've reserved a room at the hotel next to the hospital to give us a place to crash."

The speed and pitch of my speech cranked up again. I sounded like Weird Al Yankovic's *Hamilton* polka or those chipmunks from ancient history. "Okay—maybe two days? Wait, we've already got a generic go-bag by the back door. Water bottles, snacks, sunscreen—"

Nick folded his arms across his chest. "We can pass on the sunscreen. There's snow in the forecast. JD, if all you can do is panic, you're not helping your sister. She needs support."

"She might die! The baby might die!" I stuffed the phone in my pocket and kept my voice at a whisper.

"True. If that happens, do you want to remember having helped her as much as you could to the very end? Or do you want to be thrown out, missing her first moments as a mom—or worse, their last moments? If you want to panic, let me drive. At this point you're more of a wreck than I am."

I gulped. The guy with a service dog was in better shape than me? I had to say he looked like the one in control. "How do you do it?"

He let out a long breath. "The way I used to do it, before the accident, is I'd put all my personal stuff in a nearby metaphorical basket and get on with helping. I could always collapse later. Saint, say hi to JD. He needs help."

Saint plodded over and nudged me with his nose. I aimed the phone at him. "Merry, Saint says hi."

Mrs. Ly's face replaced Merry's. "We're busy now, JD. You can talk to her at the hospital."

"Merry, I love you! I'll be there soon! Here's Saint again! You'll be fine!" I kept up that nonsense for at least a minute after the screen went blank. I didn't realize I was gasping for breath after every sentence.

Saint nudged me again. I let my hand fall on his head. A drop of tension left my body.

I took the stairs to my room three at a time and scooped up my go-bag for when I travel to immigration court (minus the suit). I gave a quick pat to Havoc and her four kittens, lounging on my pillow, before darting back downstairs.

I had an ambulance to chase.

Nick, coming out of the clinic with Johnny, raised his eyebrows as I galloped down the stairs.

I declared to Nick, "I'm good to drive."

He looked me over. "Okay then. Do you have everything?"

I paused. "Yes."

Nick tried to keep a straight face. "How about a coat?"

I wasn't hitting on as many cylinders as I thought. I made it to the coat closet in three giant steps. When I reached inside, something, almost definitely a cat, scampered out and dashed toward the back of the house.

Johnny scooped up the almost-cat Godzilla. The hairless Sphynx struggled out of Johnny's arms and issued a warning hiss at Saint. The cat eyed the kitten bed. Smart Sphynx cats consent to wear a sweater or pajamas.

But he's an expert at locating the warmer places in the house. He glared at the vermin infesting the heated bed before deciding to risk it. The babies squealed and snuggled in close when he came within range. He looked alarmed when they latched on and nursed him with vigor, but he didn't throw them off either. In fact, when one kitten wandered away, Godzilla reached for it with a gentle paw and brought it back to the cuddle puddle. He licked its orange head furiously.

Johnny headed to the clinic to prepare bottles of kitten milk.

We zoomed toward San Mateo, unchecked by police. Saint sat behind me and panted—drooled—over my shoulder. Only smooth rumbles from the car on the mostly smooth highway and doggy noises met my ears, since I didn't turn on the music, the better to concentrate on the howling voices in my head.

I glanced at Nick as I whispered, "I promised to stay with her, but I sent her off in an ambulance. I feel horrible for breaking my promise, but I was glad I didn't have to continue as her birth partner."

Nick snorted. "You think people want to run into a burning building? A few weirdos do, but most of us have decided somebody needs to do this job, and it's us. You sent her with a registered nurse whom she knows. You made the best decision, to leave her in medical hands for fifteen minutes. You'll be back with her soon."

His words gave me something to yell back at the voices.

After I maneuvered the car onto I-35, Nick spoke in a quiet voice, "Do you go to San Mateo often?"

"Can't remember I've ever done so by choice. There's nothing there I can't get more of and better a few more miles up the road. All it has to offer is a branch of one of the big universities and a hospital that's closer than Austin.

The speed limit on the highway was higher than that of the back-roads, but I found myself having to slow down when I wanted to floor it. The traffic was too heavy, true about I-35 any day, any time. I bit my lip when a semi merged into my lane in front of me.

Nick grimaced a smile as he looked at his phone's GPS. "We're only a few minutes away now."

Saint snoozed against his ear for a change. Nick ruffled the dog's fur.

I silently repeated the only-a-few-minutes mantra while I sweated. I wanted to throw off my coat, impractical with the seat belt gripping me like a straitjacket.

I pulled in front of the ER entrance and jumped out. "Park the car," I hollered at Nick. "I'll see you inside."

I ran through the ER doors and made a beeline for the intake desk. Its garlands of tinsel bristled with cheerful blinking lights. "I'm Meredith Thompson's brother. Is she here yet? Can I go back with her?"

"I'll let them know you're here." This nurse was young and blonde, around Merry's age.

Her answer was inconclusive, but I called it good news. I started to ask my question again, but she'd spotted Nick.

"Excuse me, sir, is your dog a service dog?"

"Yes." He paraded Saint to show her his vest. "I'll keep him on his leash."

"Please do. He can go wherever the general public can, just stay out of the restricted areas. What is he trained to do?" She sounded like she was reading a script.

"He senses when I'm having a seizure, migraine, or panic attack. He leads me where it's safe and brings me what I need." Nick turned to me, his eyes dancing, as we took seats by the door. He whispered, "That's the only thing they can legally ask about a service dog, what he's trained to do."

I shivered inside my coat. The area by the doors was colder than the rest of the room. I sent texts to Vidal Abreu and Mrs. Ly.

Vidal appeared from the nether depths of the hospital in minutes. Tall and slim, with close-cropped, light-colored hair, he gave off an air of authority, like he ruled here. He did, I realized, a contrast from when he'd sat in my office a few months ago, begging for help.

His eyes rested on Saint, long enough to take in the service dog vest, before smiling at me. "We're admitting your sister and the baby. They seem to be doing well."

"Baby?" I gobbled. "Already?"

"Born in the ambulance. Because the baby is preterm, she's in the neonatal intensive care unit. Your sister's in recovery."

I gulped back a flood of emotions. "Thanks. Really. I didn't want Merry to give birth in our living room. I kept thinking, what if something goes wrong?"

"That's why people go to hospitals." The struggles of recent times flashed across his face. "My wife and I are thinking of moving to another state where I don't have to turn people away to miscarry in the parking lot. And our daughter is going out of state to college."

I nodded, not trusting myself to speak.

I didn't have to. The outer doors whooshed open, bringing in a blast of cold air and a group of fiery Cortezes.

"Dianne!" I squeaked in countertenor range.

CHAPTER 13

"Where is she?" Bundled to her eyebrows in a long, red hooded puffer coat and a wild-patterned scarf to rival the fourth Doctor Who's, Dianne's eyes blazed through the layers. She clenched one gloved hand, but the beads of her rosewood rosary, never far from her, peeked out. Her brother behind her resembled an enforcer.

Chaos reigned amid greetings while I caught her up with as much as I knew. I managed not to throw myself in her arms. That would be inappropriate for a business partner.

She knew Vidal and expressed her gratitude for his intervention.

He pointed out he hadn't been necessary after all. "But I did arrange for you to visit her after hours."

"Thanks." I pointed to each person to make introductions. "Vidal Abreu, administrator at San Mateo. Nick Thornton and his service dog Saint."

Saint thumped his tail and grinned.

I continued the introductions. "Dianne Cortez, my partner." I forgot the "business" part. "Zap Cortez, Dianne's younger brother. And —" I blinked as the entry doors admitted another young man. The face seemed familiar, but ... "Cortez cousin?"

"Right. Thiago Cortez." He looked to be a few years younger than

Zap, with the standard handsome Cortez features. "The family wanted me to drive because Zap and Lupita were falling apart from the time of the first text about Merry. Lupita, do you know your plans yet? I have to be back at work the day after tomorrow."

Dianne glared at him and sniffed. Her childhood nickname might have had something to do with that. "I do not fall apart, though I admit to being concerned, as was Zap. I am glad we'd reached Austin when we received your text about this hospital."

Thiago laughed. "That's why the two of you screamed the Rosary all the way. Not falling apart at all."

Dianne shoved her rosary in her pocket. She pulled her hood back and tossed her wavy black hair, standing straight out from static. "It is appropriate to offer prayers for the sick and suffering, not to mention mothers in labor."

I won't say Dianne's never prayed, because who knows what people do in the privacy of their bedrooms, but I've never known her to pray out loud when it wasn't part of a forced-attendance church service.

She raised an eyebrow at me. "JD, can we count on you for a ride back to Beauchamp, whenever you go back? I want to stay until Merry's safe, but that could be days."

"Sure," I agreed.

Thiago nodded. "In that case, I'll start for home. Can someone come with me and get your luggage?"

Nick rose to his feet and gave Saint another command. "I've still got your keys, JD. I'll put their things in your car."

"Is Merry okay?" demanded Zap. He'd been giving her fond gazes since she was in high school. Just when he'd decided she was old enough to date, she'd been attacked and fell pregnant. He'd spent the months since trying to be supportive without demanding a relationship. I hoped Merry would be able to think about such things soon, at least in time measured in weeks or months.

Vidal gave his report again as he bade us all goodbye. "Don't worry about visiting hours. You can go up as soon as she's settled in her room."

My phone rang as I thanked him.

Mrs. Ly's face, tired but happy, appeared on my screen. "JD, Merry and the baby are doing fine, but the staff wants to observe her for a little longer."

"Can I—we—come see her?" I fanned the screen around to show Mrs. Ly the crowd.

"When she's in her room, but you can talk to her now."

The phone jiggled, and when it steadied, Merry's worn-out face filled the screen.

I swallowed tears. "Are you okay, Sissy? I'm sorry I wasn't there for the main event."

"Weren't you? I thought you were right there beside me. I kept hearing your voice." She dismissed my apology with a half-inch wobble of her head. "What am I going to put on the birth certificate? 'Place of birth: Stoplight north of San Mateo'? Have you seen Jadey yet? She's beautiful!"

I went for diplomacy, never having seen an infant that ranked more than a few degrees above repulsive. Parents must be under the influence of drugs or sorcery. "I'm sure she is. Can we see her? We're in the ER lobby. Besides Nick and Saint, there's Dianne and Zap."

Merry covered her face. "Don't let Zap see me! Not like this."

Zap called over my shoulder, "Dulce amiga, you will never be anything but beautiful, as beautiful as the Blessed Mother with her child on Christmas."

Dianne knocked me away with one side blow from her hip, a move perfected by years of dancing. "Chica, we came as fast as we could!"

I handed her my phone and backed away, not quite limping. "Dulce amiga," Zap said. Literally "sweet friend," like "friend zone" in the US. Poor guy.

"Dianne!" sobbed Merry.

I turned when the doors behind me wheezed open again. I called above Dianne's blandishments, "Merry, Cherry and the grandparents are here."

Cherry threw her arms around my neck in something like a hug, but fiercer. "I'm glad you were with her. I wanted to be—but I'm glad I missed it."

I hugged her back, not as hard. "I know exactly what you mean."

Dianne held up my phone, and the new arrivals swarmed around it.

Nick having returned, I returned to my seat beside him. He looked pained.

He lifted his eyes to the ceiling. "So *this* is what family acts like. Amazing."

My phone chirped. I glanced at it. "*Your* family still amazes *me*. Then and now. Here's another text from Jessa."

Nick sighed. "Jessa."

"She's begging me to contact you or give her the names of anybody who might know where you are. They had to take your father to the Emergency Room, and she says he has something to say to you before he dies."

Nick scowled. "And I'm supposed to care why? It's too late to apologize for turning me loose on my own to scramble my way into adulthood." Sharp, hard breaths punctuated each phrase. "Besides, doesn't that sound like the kind of prank Jessa would pull?"

Grim memories surfaced. "It does, but it's been years since I've heard from her at all."

Saint stood up and put his head in Nick's lap.

"Yeah, boy. I'm fine. I will be, anyway. You're the best part of my life." Nick leaned over and buried his face in Saint's fur.

I shook my head. "I still can't figure out why your father threw you out. I mean, you came out when you were twelve."

He sat up straight. "I don't know. Mamí insisted they'd love me no matter what. Dad went along with her, but he wasn't happy about it. But she left not even a year later, and we never heard from her again. I always felt like I had something to do with that."

"I'm sure her leaving had nothing to do with you. I tell my divorcing clients to make sure their kids know it's not their fault."

"What are you, a social worker? Dad throwing me out five years later, saying he had to protect his stepchildren, was nuts too. He'd been married to my stepmother Crystal for two years, and I thought I got along okay with her. Heck, I was dating Angelica then, being as straight as I could." He sighed and sagged. "She broke up with me right after that too. Nothing made any sense. Life generally doesn't, I've found. Now Crystal's dead and my father's dying. Still crazy."

"You've never heard from them, more than ten years now?"

Nick sighed so deep it sounded like a groan. "After they missed our Eagle ceremony, prom, and high school graduation, why would they turn up for anything else?"

Nick had buckled down to reach Eagle rank with me and three others in the troop. Mother put together the Court of Honor at our Methodist Church. The Jewish scouts said it was as big as a bar mitzvah, which I took as a compliment.

Local schools and organizations used the church's Fellowship Hall as an event center. With our guest list of family, friends, and anyone we'd ever spoken to, we crammed it full enough that no one noticed Nick's lack of guests.

Except Nick.

He went missing before the Court of Honor. Our scout master told us our last requirement was to organize a search for Nick, as though he were lost in the woods, and bring him back.

I found him ten minutes later sitting on the steps of the front entrance. He hugged his knees and said he was waiting for his family in case they showed up and didn't know where to go. He'd sent them an invitation.

He seemed ready to sit there all night. I suggested we make a sign with a map and post it on the door.

He thought about it. "How about on all the entrances?"

I rounded up the other Eagles, and our last requirement turned out to be making posters for each church entrance with a map to the Fellowship Hall, just in case all the church signs pointing that way were insufficient.

Spoiler: No one from his family showed. During the ceremony, my parents acted as his parents, and we shared my grandfather as our special speaker. No one minded having one less speech to sit through.

Mother conspired with the other mothers to make sure Nick had as many gifts on the table as the favored sons whose family showed up. It wasn't hard; for his Eagle project, he made pint-sized furniture for the church's new preschool wing. People in the congregation were happy to support him. During the reception, they kidnapped other guests to give them tours of Nick's work. I hope that was a comfort to him or at least spared him some humiliation. He started smiling about three-quarters of the way through the evening.

CHAPTER 14

Nick fiddled with Saint's leash, pulling it through his fingers over and over. "After the Court of Honor, I was done. If I didn't invite them to anything, I couldn't be disappointed when they didn't show."

"I can understand why you wouldn't reach out again." A glance at his stony face told me he was lying. "Your family is going in my Parental Hall of Infamy. Even with my few years of law practice, the competition is fierce."

Dianne left my phone with Cherry and took the chair on the other side of me. "They're taking Merry to her room now. We'll be able to see her soon."

Because she'd killed our conversation, I deflected. "Been meaning to ask you. Can we hire our intern to come back to work early, even part time? Johnny has a new injured mom cat with five kittens."

She looked at me like I'd shape-shifted into something unrecognizable. Maybe I had.

In a stilted, unpracticed tone, she thanked me for my consideration. "Do I have this right? You're asking me rather telling me you've already called him?"

Guilt-ridden, I shrank down in my seat. My face turned hot as I remembered other occasions when I'd made financial commitments—

for good and charitable reasons—and expected her to untangle them. When Cherry summoned us to the elevator, I sprang up, relieved.

Merry's floor was guarded by a long, tall desk with a pocket-sized Christmas tree on one end, a menorah on the other, though both holidays were over. Secular snow scenes separated them. The attending nurse-dragon wanted to throw us out.

I flexed my legal vocal cords. "Mr. Abreu gave us permission for relaxed visitors' hours."

The nurse glared at me through the snowmen before her. "He said her brother."

"I'm her brother. Nick's her foster brother. Dianne's my partner. Zap is *her* brother. Cherry is Merry's twin sister. The Thompsons are our grandparents. Mrs. Ly is her personal medical attendant. I can't think of anyone who shouldn't be here."

Mrs. Ly emerged from Merry's room. "We need to work out our schedule for people to stay with her tonight and tomorrow."

The nurse frowned. "That isn't necessary."

"If we need permission from Mr. Abreu, he'll give it." She disappeared back into Merry's room. We tried to follow, but half our group had to stand in the hall.

Merry lay exhausted in bed but somehow bristling with excitement. "I'm going to see my baby!"

We all murmured happy things.

"I will sleep on the window-seat bed." Mrs. Ly gestured toward the window, which had a cushion long and wide enough for an average-sized man to sleep on.

It looked uncomfortable, and I wasn't approaching seventy years old. "We'll book more rooms at the hotel, Mrs. Ly."

"I'd rather be nearby." Mrs. Ly stood up and eyed a new nurse, trying to reach Merry's bedside with a wheelchair. "I know the staff is busy."

Merry set her chin, firmly tilted at that twin-specific angle. "I want my baby baptized."

I wanted her to have everything she wanted for the rest of her life. "Sure. In Houston or—?"

"Now." Her voice held firm.

I met the eyes of the nurse. "I'm sure they have a chaplain."

The nurse, five-foot nothing in a Size 2 uniform, maybe graduating from middle school soon, shook her head. "We used to, but with budget cutbacks—we have ministers who volunteer." She looked doubtful.

"In the middle of the night?" I looked at Merry doubtfully, hoping she didn't have a premonition of anyone's death. We hadn't grown up with the concept of infant baptism.

Merry's chin quivered. She raised it higher.

Dianne pushed through from the hall. "This is my jam. I trained for this moment ever since Sister Immaculata told us that any confirmed Catholic could act as a priest in emergency situations. I'm calling this an emergency."

I aimed a lopsided grin at her. "Trained?"

She flashed me an imperious look. "I baptized every Barbie in the house."

My grin widened, imagining young Dianne and the Barbies. "Not the Kens?"

"I did Anointing of the Sick for the Kens."

"I want that for Jadey too," Merry announced.

"You shall have it." Dianne pulled off her coat and tossed it on the windowsill. She arranged her long, wild scarf like a clergyman's stole. It hung down symmetrically over her shoulders and down her burgundy sweater dress, now playing the part of a cassock. "Zap, go get some oil and a bottle of water from the cafeteria. Everyone who wants to be part of this show, meet in front of the preemie nursery in 10 minutes."

"On it." With a last smile at Merry, Zap set his shoulders like a football player and shoved through the crowd.

Now I understood the expression "wreathed in smiles." That's how Merry looked, her first genuine smile of the day.

Merry turned her smile to the family. "Granny, Cherry, JD, I want you to be godparents."

Cherry twisted her hands. "I'll do anything you want, but shouldn't a godparent know something about God?"

Nick's voice came from in the hall, where he stood with Saint. "I know something about God."

Grandmother laid a hand on Cherry's arm. "I too will do anything you want, Merry, but I feel my age is a disadvantage."

I cleared my throat. "I will too, Merry. But you've named all family members. You know we'll help. This is a great opportunity to reach out for more support. Remember baptisms at our Methodist church, when the minister asked the congregation to take godparent vows? If you do it that way, then everybody who wants to can make the responses."

I didn't think it was possible for Merry to smile bigger, but she did. Everyone in the room and watching from the door beamed along with her.

I moved closer to Dianne to murmur, "Isn't Anointing of the Sick also called Last Rites?"

She didn't look up, being busy flicking through her phone in search of the ceremonies. "Not since before our parents were born. Catch up, JD."

"You're the expert." The room emptied around me. I stepped forward to push Merry's wheelchair, but her nurse stared me down. I stepped out of her way and followed like a six-foot-three page boy. I should have carried a long train or a pillow with a ring.

When we arrived at the neonatal unit, the rest of our crew were pressed against the nursery window and making silly noises at the babies. Everyone fell back to let Merry be as close as possible. I expect the nurse's gimlet gaze had something to do with it.

I grinned when I could see through the crowd. Grandmother sat at a spindly keyboard on wheels. If there's a piano equivalent in the county, she will find it. A long-haired young guy hung over her—or it—protectively as she played quiet songs from the Methodist hymnal. Nick stood some feet away from her. Saint, still on his leash, lay by Nick with an uninterested expression.

Cold weather static had shaped Dianne's wavy black hair into a dark halo, making her taller than me. Despite her colorful vestments, she'd taken on even more gravitas than normal. She let her rosewood rosary trail through her fingers as she held her phone like a religious book.

Though her mother named her Guadalupe Dianne Cortez y Jáquez and dedicated her to Mexico's Virgin of Guadalupe, when Dianne pulled herself up straight, pale brown eyes blazing, she reminded me more of Quetzalcoatl, the older Mexican deity whose image graced most of her belongings, including her phone case. If Dianne was imploring both the feathered serpent and the golden Virgin, this child was guaranteed maximum protection and blessing.

Dianne conferred in quiet Spanish with the nursery attendant through the speaker.

Stepping back, she announced, "The baby nurse is Catholic too. She'll mirror what I'm doing on this side of the window, even though she won't have the oil and water." She wrinkled her nose as Zap held up his offerings. "Which is just as well because really, Zap, Italian salad dressing?"

He lifted his shoulders and let them fall. "Best I could do in a hospital cafeteria at this hour."

Dianne took a few seconds to gather herself. "Thank you. It's better than motor oil, I suppose. Stand beside me and act as my altar boy. I can't hold all the elements at the same time."

Zap opened the bottle and package. The dressing's vinegar-herbal bouquet wafted through the air, more pleasant than the hospital cleaning chemicals. I suspected I'd now approach salad bars with an urge to genuflect, like I do when the aroma of incense hits my nostrils.

Dianne frowned at her phone. "I will read the service close to the way it's written. I don't want to get into a theological discussion." She scowled at me. I raised my hands in surrender.

I tapped my phone. "Hang on a second. Johnny will want to be part of this. If you want him, Merry."

His grandmother, seated on her rolling walker, twitched her mouth into a smile. "A Jewish Buddhist as a godparent?"

"Yes!" Merry affirmed.

I smiled at both as I tapped his number. "We can't have too many helpers, and best to cover all bases."

Johnny, still working in his clinic, was honored. I flipped my phone around to show him what was happening.

"Dearly beloved, we gather here in joy to welcome this child as ... as a gift from God." Dianne stumbled over the words. Anything less joyful than this child's beginnings was hard to imagine. She continued, stronger, "What name do you give your child?"

"Jade Adrienne Arline Thompson," answered Merry in definite tones that dwindled when answering Dianne's next questions. She hadn't studied for the exam.

Dianne cleared her throat and declaimed, "You have asked to have Jade Adrienne Arline baptized. It will be your duty to bring her up to keep God's commandments as Christ taught us, by loving God and our neighbor. Do you clearly understand what you are undertaking?"

"I—I think so." Merry looked terrified. At Dianne's whispered coaching, she replied, "Yes. I do."

Dianne turned her Quetzalcoatl eyes around the room and demanded, "Are you ready to help the mother of this child in her duty as a Christian parent?"

Amid the murmurs—and a yip from Saint—the courtroom voice of Jay Thompson rang out, "I do."

I whipped my head around and gaped in astonishment, both at our father's presence and his participation. He and Mallory stood back a few feet from us, closer to the elevator than to the nursery. She held his arm like she was holding him up. I saw her lips moving as well.

My stomach fell somewhere around my knees. They must be serious, if she was making promises for his granddaughter.

Amid the scriptures, Dianne exhorted us to a faithful life, with the implication that she'd be checking up on us. She made motions—Sign of the Cross?—in the air with oil and then water. The nurse at little Jade's side made similar motions over the tiny child.

So very tiny! We'd passed the regular nursery on our way here. The contrast between those plump butterballs and these scraps of humanity broke my heart. My responses to Dianne's demands for prayer surprised me by being loud as my father's.

As Dianne moved into a brisk version of the Anointing of the Sick, I made my way to the piano. To let Grandmother keep the chair, I moved the keyboard away at an angle and played standing up. The young man guarding the piano helped me adjust it.

Dianne, looking exhausted, burned me with her eyes as she pronounced the last Amen. I flashed her a slight smile with one shake of my head. She didn't have to be part of this gig.

I rippled quiet arpeggios as I sang the second verse of ABBA's "My

Love, My Life" from the second *Mamma Mia* movie, the baptism song that's reduced every mother and child to tears. With the late—early—hour, I figured we didn't need more than one verse. I hadn't a prayer of hitting the high note at the end, but I was willing to try.

Sure enough, sniffles rose from the audience before the end of the first phrase. By the second, Dianne had made her way to my side. She dropped a hand on my shoulder as she contributed a soft harmony, surprising me as much as did the ghost-grandmother in the movie. When Dianne claimed the high note before I could embarrass myself, my eyes misted up.

"Go in peace," she proclaimed after the note died away.

CHAPTER 15

To avoid all the people I came with, I turned to the guardian of the piano and thanked him in earnest tones. Before the baptism, after Dianne dispensed us to prepare, Grandmother had gone hunting for a piano, finding a cheap electric version stamped as hospital property in the chapel. She and Grandfather had rolled it halfway down the hall before he caught up with them.

He'd been sleeping in the chapel, hiding from hospital staff. He planned to play for his brother's wedding in the chapel the next day and became alarmed when the piano left.

Of course the grandparents were polite when he tried to reclaim the instrument. Of course they could use it for their great-granddaughter's baptism. Of course they would take good care of it and return it in the same pristine condition. If they were onsite tomorrow, they would love to attend his cancer-ridden brother's wedding.

It's the South. What can I say?

Thank you very much, sir. You're so kind. We deeply appreciate it. And I would be happy to play and sing an ABBA song for the event. Probably the lovely lady would too.

Such is the grease of life in these parts. Grinning at everyone's totally typical behavior dried my eyes.

After the baptism, with a last wave and mutual good wishes, he wheeled the piano away. I bet he'd tie the piano to his ankle to prevent another theft.

My people still looked beatific and uplifted as they murmured how lovely the ceremony was. Saint looked the same way while crunching the treat Nick gave him.

Merry turned in her wheelchair to press against the glass, like it would give way to admit her to her baby's side. Her nurse tried to push her toward the elevator, but Merry clung to the glass like a remora.

"You can see your baby tomorrow—later today—after you rest," said the nurse, who despite her honeyed voice, reminded me of the high school coach who made us run up and down the bleachers for the entire PE hour.

Merry wilted in her wheelchair as the fatigue of the day and night caught up with her. How could she not be beyond exhausted? She cast a yearning glance toward the baby.

We all wandered in a random Brownian motion back to Merry's room, giving the medical people a chance to look her over privately. Mrs. Ly stayed right by her side, though, which comforted me.

I put an arm around Dianne. "That was fantastic. I never knew how involved you were with your church."

Her eyes held a steely glint. "My grandmothers used to say that any day now, the Church would admit women priests. Turns out they were wrong, and once I figured that out, I was done with the Church as an institution."

"You're definitely the High Priestess of Gregg House."

She turned to me, her light brown eyes with the golden flecks boring into mine. "I don't know any spiritual language besides Church language, but I know it's important to stand with people at the edge, the edge of birth or death, of crossing over or coming back. Like a gatekeeper."

I gulped and asked the question gnawing on my mind all night. Mrs. Ly's words about Jade being "on the edge of viability" kept coming back to me. "Do you know which is happening?"

"No. Gatekeepers don't get to know. You just do your job. You hold the door open, but you don't decide who goes through it or when." She sounded frustrated, like she really did want to know.

Life as normal then. "As you did. Got any brujas in your family?"

"Like my mother would permit a sorceress among us." Her voice dropped lower in pitch and volume. "Tía Valeria."

The elevator dinged in response, the only sound in the hall. We walked in silence to Merry's room. As we approached, soft strains of song in an unfamiliar language from an unaccompanied tenor voice met our ears.

Dianne smiled. "Johnny."

The ends of my lips curved up in a mirror of hers. "'Mi Shebeirach,' the healing prayer he sings while he's working in the clinic."

"Appropriate."

When we reached the room, the hospital staff was breaking away from Merry, lying so still on the bed. Mrs. Ly held my phone out to me, and I pushed in to reclaim it. Johnny was finishing the second verse of his song.

"Thank you, Johnny. That was beautiful." Merry's skin looked translucent but glowing.

Dianne spoke into the phone. "Johnny, if you want to call in our intern to help out until we get back, that's fine with me."

I touched her back in appreciation and moved to Merry's side to clasp her hand.

Slumping in the window seat cushion, Mrs. Ly spoke in firm accents to those with medical training. They would monitor Merry and take her vital signs in two-hour shifts. As an EMT with the most training of anyone except Mrs. Ly, Nick and Saint had the first shift. Zap as a Dallas Parks employee and Mallory as a librarian had first aid training.

Mrs. Ly's face had gone gray with exhaustion. "With me and maybe JD, who learned a lot yesterday, that gives us ten hours of medical supervision."

I started in surprise at my promotion.

As the medical crew broke away, Mrs. Ly said to the rest of the room. "We'll set up a visitation schedule for non-medical people too. We don't want to overcrowd the room. I'll be sleeping on the windowsill cushion. Wake me if her numbers change."

I elbowed my way to Mrs. Ly and whispered, "Let me take you to the hotel."

Her eyes flashed. "We're close to saving both of them, JD. The baby is receiving expert care. Merry's fever is going down, but I want to be on the spot if her condition changes." She closed her eyes and spoke even softer. "Some hospitals forbid the use of certain medications because they're used in abortions, and mothers bleed out."

"What!" I'd spoken louder than I meant to. I went back to a zero-level volume. "There's no question of abortion. She's given birth." Had I fallen into a Lewis Carroll down-the-rabbit-hole version of medicine?

Her lips tugged up in a smile of pure winter. "You keep expecting things to make sense." She looked down at her medical bag. I realized she'd never let go of it in the hospital. "But I'm prepared for any contingency."

I blinked in sudden understanding. "Thank you. Call me if you get in trouble."

Her brown eyes danced among wrinkles of amusement. "I assume legal representation is part of our landlord-tenant agreement."

"Of course," I promised.

"Dad, why don't you sit with Merry while I take the Grands to the hotel?" Cherry called from the doorway. "Then I'll sit with her as part of the non-medical crew."

He jerked toward the bed like somebody pushed him. Maybe it was true, since Mallory was standing behind him.

Merry teared up. "Daddy!"

He stood rigid, eyes bulging, like a taxidermist's pet project—in other words, his usual response to emotional situations.

"There, there," I coached him. I put Merry's hand in his. How come I know more about being a father than he does?

CHAPTER 16

People wandered off in their own groups. I headed to the cafeteria to get food for Nick, since he had first watch over Merry.

I made a detour by the chapel, shrouded in darkness. It must have had windows, because outdoor lights gleamed on the far side of the room. A table-shaped lump might have been an altar. The only object I could definitely identify was the piano, parked near the door, which I shut softly. I don't know who I imagined I might disturb, but one doesn't make a noise in church.

But I did, with a voice that rang in the small room. "You didn't save my mother, the only prayer of my teenage years, but I swear, if my sister or her baby dies, I am done with You forever."

A shocked face popped up from behind a chair. With effort, I recognized the guardian of the piano.

"Everything okay, man?" he asked.

As best I could see in the shadows, he looked frightened. Given my oratory, I could understand that.

I waved a hand. "I'm worried about my sister. Her baby. You saw them."

"Yeah, man. I did. I'll pray for them, okay?"

"Thanks. And I'll pray for your ... brother?" I saw him nod. "Why are you sleeping in here?"

"I was going to sleep in my truck, but it's cold. Security never does anything but open the door and look in."

"Listen, go to the hotel across the street and tell them you're with the Thompson party. Let me know if they give you any trouble. You've got my number." I was going to have to find out who was paying.

"Thanks. I didn't realize I'd be here so many days. Remember, I'll be praying for you." He folded his space blanket. It flashed in the weak light. He put it in a backpack.

"Me too. For you, I mean. And your family." Feeling awkward, I backed out of the room.

I delivered Nick's food and told him to call me if he wanted a ride later. He said the day he couldn't walk across the street, he'd get a wheelchair for Saint to pull. It did seem silly to drive across the street, but sillier to park around the clock in the hospital lot. Besides, the air was frigid, with a tease of snow. I eased my car into the hotel parking lot.

A familiar figure in red danced in the hotel unloading zone. Dianne has had training in multiple dance forms, but she looks best just letting her limbs fly in spontaneous movements and skippety-hopping however she feels. I could almost put a song to her locomotion; I knew music played in her mind. I savored the sight for a moment and then joined her, keeping my distance until she pulled off her scarf and roped me in close.

She breathed warm, tickling words into my ear. "I'm trying to ground myself. I feel like I'm about to fly away."

I pulled her in closer and then launched her into a spin. She made it a triple, laughing the whole time. I dipped, spun, and turned her until she whisked herself into my arms and planted the biggest kiss of all time on me. I pulled her close enough to squeeze the air out of her coat. Who says dreams can't come true?

We'd danced outside the sheltering overhang, and needles of precipitation stabbed my cheeks and eyelids, the only skin uncovered. I kissed her corresponding body parts, those also under assault by the droplets we call a Texas snowstorm.

"Sorry!" she gasped. "I should have asked."

"Until I tell you definitively otherwise," I grumbled between kisses, "you have consent to do whatever—" I made my way down to her neck. "—you want. Please."

After something between a moan and a sigh, that slight, she murmured, "With Mallory in the picture, I thought I'd have to ask permission to say good morning."

"That picture's shattered." The occasion called for more kisses, fiercely returned. "Do you have a roommate tonight?"

"Yes. Mallory."

I jumped back like she'd tossed a bucket of cold water. "Mallory? Why didn't you put her with my father?"

"She took over acquiring and assigning rooms and asked me if I'd stay with her. With my mind whirling after the ceremonies, I didn't mind, just glad I wasn't making the decisions. Let's go inside. It's cold out here."

The hotel entrance doors parted to admit us, and she went to the front desk to get her keycard. When she returned, I asked, "Who am I sleeping with?"

She pulled out her phone to check. "Your father."

I made an astonished, appalled noise, but the entry door behind us whooshed open to admit Mallory. I stepped away from them both.

"Thanks for arranging the rooms." I might have sounded sarcastic. I tried again. "I guess you're the one to thank for getting my father here?"

Mallory pushed back her coat's hood and then her hair. Someone should invent a hairstyle that looks good in winter static. "Arline, Jim, and Cherry took off after one of your texts. Jay kept asking me, 'What should I do?' I told him he should go to his daughter. He just stared at me. After your update from the Brampton hospital, I walked him toward the door. He said, 'She doesn't want to see me.' I said that was irrelevant. He said, 'You're right. She might need my insurance information.'"

"Sounds just like him," I admitted. "I thought we'd have to hogtie him to get him to her baby shower a few weeks ago, and that was supposed to be a happy event. My mother did all the emotional stuff. He paid the bills."

She shrugged her shoulders and spread her hands wide, like a plea to heaven. "It's been a day. I'm glad Merry and the baby are okay. So far. My shift with her starts at eight. I'm going to get some sleep." She headed for the elevator.

"Good idea," Dianne agreed as she followed.

"Sweet dreams," I called.

When the door shut behind them, I stood there stewing in my emotions. Suddenly the opposite of exhausted, I headed back to my car. I was furious with my father, Mallory, Texas politics, and the universe that dropped me in this night's nightmare. "Why Did It Have to Be Me," indeed.

I needed a drink. Multiple drinks. Jimmy Buffet's boat drinks, something to keep me warm in this frigid weather. But Texas bars close at 2:00 a.m. The only way I'd get a drink would be to buy a six-pack at a convenience store and drink it in my room. Gee, with my dad? What a bonding experience. The thought made me nauseous.

Food sounded good. Pursuing it would get me away from everyone. My phone told me about a nearby twenty-four-hour diner called Gina's, not that anything in San Mateo was far away from anything else. For example, this downtown restaurant was only three miles away from the hospital on the northern edge of town.

Downtown was as dead as my love life. A weak light shone from Gina's, not beckoning, more like "Okay, if you have to." I pulled into one of the angled parking spots in front. A sign said I could find more parking in the back. Maybe Gina's had a lunch rush.

The squat, two-story, stone building that housed the restaurant straddled the line between vintage and dilapidated. That was obvious even without the "Established 1958" neon sign. The vinyl booths, some repaired with duct tape, were empty. Round, red vinyl stools with shiny metal bases lined up in front of the counter. One woman in an old-fashioned pink uniform stood behind it.

A chalkboard begged you to try the award-winning pies with an old-fashioned ice-cream soda or milkshake. An all-glass, old-fashioned bakery case stood forlorn and empty. I felt like a time traveler, walking into a historical diner, lit with yellow-tinged lights like an Edward Hopper painting.

Because I could feel the cold leaching out from the big windows overlooking the street, I sat in the back booth, the only one not pressed against the front windows. No sooner had I lowered my rear on the seat than the slim, dark-haired server bustled to the table.

"What can I get—"

"I'll have a—"

We stared at each other.

"JD Thompson! Second trombone, Lamar High School orchestra!" she exclaimed.

"Angelica Rossi, second flute!" I replied in wonder. Nick's high school girlfriend.

She laughed, and the lights glinted on the red in her dark auburn hair, wound into a net-covered bun that revealed classically beautiful features, a straight but delicate nose. "*First* flute by the time I graduated, a year after you did."

I remembered the war for first chair flute. On audition day, Angelica had dowsed herself with a vile perfume, bringing on an allergic reaction from Rachel, the defending first chair and a senior. All to no avail: the conductor allowed Rachel to play another day, and she kept the chair. I hoped Angelica had improved since then.

She pointed to her name tag. "It's Angelica Thornton now."

My brain struggled to process that information. "You married ..."

"Brett Thornton. He was Brett Holland in high school, before his stepfather adopted him."

CHAPTER 17

Brett Holland, now Thornton.

Angelica broke up with Nick around the time he came to live with my family. Then she dated and married his step-brother? I had questions, lots of them, but I thought I'd get more information by listening.

Angelica gave me a server's smile. "Our specialties are baked desserts. I just took a blackberry cobbler out of the oven. Would you like some? It goes great with ice cream. We have Blue Bell Natural Vanilla Bean."

"The best! I'll have both, but I'd like your Texas Traditional breakfast too—eggs scrambled, both bacon and sausage, and biscuits—with coffee." Another memory lit up on my sagging brain board. "You used to bring pies and cobblers to our band-orchestra picnics. You said they were from your grandparents' restaurant, someday to be yours."

She laughed, pleased. "You remembered!"

"They were good!"

"The blackberries are locally sourced, picked just yesterday."

I grinned. "From your backyard, amirite? But in December?"

She mirrored my grin. "Spoken like a Native Texan. And yes, they are. My granddad's backyard where he set up a greenhouse around the time I was born. We have fresh berries and veggies through the winter."

"Smart man, your grandfather."

She beamed. "He is! I used to spend summers with my grandparents from the time I was old enough to crawl. By the time I could stand, I was bringing silverware and napkins to customers. I started baking biscuits when I was ten and desserts when I was twelve. I always wanted to run this restaurant, and Granddad was thrilled, because none of his children did. I'm glad Brett supports my dream."

Though she smiled, beneath the surface glowed a steam-rolling determination. If Brett was smart—not that he ever impressed me that way—he'd get on board or get out of the way.

Angelica brought the cobbler and ice cream as soon as I crunched the last rasher of bacon. I closed my eyes when I took the first bite. The creamy deep vanilla lit up my tastebuds. It slid soft as silk down my gullet, which begged for more.

And the blackberries! Dark, tart, sweet, just like the ones I picked as a child from the bushes in our backyard. My mother made cobblers from those berries, fresh off the vine. My father grumped about how wild the vines grew, as bad as kudzu, a constant threat to a suburban yard, but he gobbled the cobblers and pies as enthusiastically as the rest of us. When I was old enough to do yard work, he put me to trimming as well as picking the blackberries, but I didn't mind, not once I learned how to avoid the thorns.

I quit ordering cobblers in restaurants a few years ago when I concluded that the fruit had bounced around the world for a few weeks and the cook had sought to ameliorate the damage with a bucket of sugar. In contrast, my mother measured her sugar in tablespoons. Angelica hadn't added any more sugar than my mother did, and the burst of blackberry taste took me back to days of yore, washed happy by time.

Angelica looked around the empty room. Her voice had turned shy. "Mind if I sit down? I'd like to catch up."

"I'm having a religious experience from your cobbler. Now I remember you brought one to my last band-orchestra picnic before senior year. You were dating Nick Thornton then, and he helped you. We had more desserts than ever. Not that there were any leftovers."

Her expression slammed shut. Her voice turned frigid as the weather. "Of course, I broke up with him as soon as I knew."

I stirred the ice cream into the cobbler and raised a questioning eyebrow.

Her lips thinned to a straight line. "It's not my story to tell, if you don't already know." She forced the ends of those lips up into a fake smile.

I let the silence hang heavy, in case she felt inclined to fill it. I'd savored three more bites, when she looked out the window and fell back on the old Texas conversational standby.

"Do you think we'll get snow? It was in the forecast. I didn't know whether I should try to drive home or stay here. The second floor has a bedroom. Granddad keeps meaning to rent it out, but it's useful, like when the waitstaff can't find childcare. Or for naps for me when I'm baking in the early hours and then working the breakfast and lunch rushes." Her voice had a brittle edge to it.

I let her escape. "I saw a few flakes earlier, but not now. Cold, yes, but a hard, bright cold without clouds. Unless things change—always a possibility in Texas—I'd expect tomorrow to be sunny with blue skies, the kind of day that fools you into going out without a coat. We get a lot of those here in Central Texas, more than where we grew up. You should be fine going home. But shouldn't the owner or owner's granddaughter have a better shift?"

She still had to force her smile. "I like it. I get the baking done before the breakfast crowd comes in. Since we're not on the highway, we don't have many customers in the late night, just a small rush after the bars close that I can handle by myself."

"Have you been in San Mateo long?"

"No, we just moved here a few weeks ago. My dad wanted me to get through college. I earned a BS/MS degree in Global Hospitality from the University of Houston." She straightened her shoulders in pride.

I murmured admiration.

"Then Granddad thought I should get experience in other restaurants, and Brett had his job, marketing with a sports swag firm. But after his mother died, he wanted to get away from Houston. I've never seen him that broken up, not even when ..."

I wondered what other tragedy Brett had in his life. His mother's divorce? Her later marriage to Nick's dad? I smiled with all the empathy I had, but I didn't draw any more confidences from her.

Instead, her voice hardened. "I was glad when Granddad said we could come here and start work. Brett too, though Granddad doesn't much like Brett's marketing ideas. But it's a good thing we came, because both my grandparents started having health issues."

"Nothing serious, I hope." I scooped up the last bit of cobbler, mostly ice cream soup, where one juicy blackberry lurked. Delicious.

"I don't think so, but we're not sure yet. The symptoms sound a lot like Brett's parents, abdominal issues and leg cramps no one's been able to diagnose other than 'You're getting old.' Makes Granddad furious, especially when they want him to change his diet. He figures he should be healthier than anybody, as many years as he's prepared his own food." Her brows contracted more with every sentence.

A vague memory poked me. What had Johnny said about the Thorntons? I remarked, "After a lifetime of standing on hard floors, I'm not surprised your grandfather has leg problems."

"Granddad laughed at me when I first bought anti-fatigue mats for everybody in the kitchen and behind the counter. Not anymore, though." She flashed her server's smile again, banishing the dark cloud of her grandparents' health. "What are you doing these days? Do you live in San Mateo?"

"I have a law practice in Beauchamp, up the road a way. My sister Merry just had a premature baby, in the middle of the night, like babies do. The whole family is camping out in the hotel by the hospital. I'm not sure how long I'll be in San Mateo."

"If you get a chance, come in again and I'll make up a New Mother's basket. Tell me about the mother and baby."

"Thanks. That's kind of you. Baby is Jade Adrienne Arline, almost three pounds now. Peppermint and lemon are Merry's favorite flavors, if that makes a difference. Not together."

"I bet you had a lemon tree in your backyard in West U."

"Wasn't that a law? We did, and a black cherry tree too for my sister Cherry."

A bell dinged from the kitchen, and Angelica ran back after another flash of a smile. I lounged by the cash register at the counter until she returned, smelling of fresh pecan pie. She handed me a piece in a transparent box but wouldn't let me pay for it. I added the price to her tip, already large, because of the unwritten law about old high school friends. It's the South.

CHAPTER 18

The still, crisp early morning, as dark as a town ever gets, contributed to my otherworldly state while I drove back to the hotel. Drunks had gone home, and the early risers weren't yet on the road. If I were Franz Grüber, I might have written "Silent Night," but with a backbeat, to update it.

The sight of the hotel reminded me that I was booked for the night into a room with my father. That was the final straw for a horrible day. It seemed all in a day's work to help my friend vacate his home, drive my laboring sister across the state, act as her birth coach, take part in a bizarre baptism, dance with Dianne, and run into Nick's high school flame. But no one could expect me to sleep in the same room as my father.

Yet they did.

To avoid the sight of the hotel and what it held for me, I looked across the street at the hospital. A massive blob squatted in the front lawn. Saint was doing his business while Nick leaned against a light post.

I angled the car in their direction. By the time I caught up to him, he'd picked up Saint's leavings, thrown them in a trash can, and limped a few steps toward the street.

I rolled down the car window and yelled, "Want a ride?"

When he turned, I saw exhaustion carved in his face with a chain saw. "It's just across the street, and Saint needs the exercise."

"Tell you what. You drive the car. I'll walk the dog, if he'll come with me."

Nick gave up fast. "He will if I tell him to. Go walkies with JD, Saint."

As we changed places, Nick told me Merry was sleeping soundly with all her numbers holding steady. Baby Jade was doing well in the NICU. He drove off before I had my coat snapped and my gloves on, hard to do with Saint tugging on the leash. He wanted to catch up with his guy. When we reached the hotel parking lot, Saint broke into a gallop to greet Nick getting out of the car.

Nick knelt slower than usual to give his dog a hug.

I accepted the keys he held out. "Do you have a roommate?"

"How would I know?"

"If one of our well-meaning planners informed you."

He checked his phone. "Here's something from someone named Mallory."

I ground my chattering teeth.

"She says she didn't give me a roommate because Saint and I might like the extra space."

"Is that true? Or could I crash on the other bed?"

"Who's your roommate?"

"My dad. I swear, Nick, I'll get my own room before I'll share with him. My last nerve has been whittled down to a carbon chain filament."

"You can stay with us. I'd rather have someone nearby I can call if things get bad." He reached in the car and came up with my bag and the pie box. "Should I take this pie inside?"

"Sure. Do you want it?"

His face lit up like Christmas. But he was still a public servant. "Split it?"

"I just had breakfast and blackberry cobbler. Leave me a commission, like ten percent."

"Thanks! I'm too beat to go out, but I'm starved."

"That's a traditional Texas breakfast. You want me to get us some beer or wine at whatever's open?"

"Only if you want. I've got a date with a pain pill. Drinking's not advised."

"Nah, I don't need any booze." I looked down at Saint who raised his eyebrows with, I swear, skepticism. "I am *not* lying. I do not *need* alcohol. But if you were my dog, you'd be carrying a brandy cask around your neck like your ancestors."

Nick laughed as he turned toward the hotel's front doors with Saint by his side. I followed them.

The warm air of the hotel hit my cheeks like a blast from a furnace —or a fire, as my screaming brain reminded me, though the resemblance to my traumatic fire experience was slight. PTSD: fun for the ages.

The small establishment teetered between the two- and three-star level. A minimal chance of bedbugs, a reasonable expectation of cleanliness, maybe even quiet. The kind of place the immigration nonprofit I work for would book for me.

Nick handed me my room card, and we crowded into the elevator. In the room, he released Saint from his leash. The dog bounded up on Nick's queen-sized bed.

Nick sat on the bed and propped all his pillows behind him. When he'd raised himself high enough, he tore into the pie. His expression felt familiar. "Where did you get this? Can we go there for lunch or whenever our next meal is?"

I pulled off my gloves and coat and took time to consider. "At a little local place called Gina's."

I wondered how much to tell him. Surely Nick could avoid Angelica by going in the daytime, if she liked working the graveyard shift. But did his stepbrother work in the restaurant during the day?

"Gina's." Nick's voice went flat as Angelica's pancakes.

"Yeah. It's one of those vintage diners, founded in 1958."

His voice grew colder. "By the Rossi family."

"Right."

"I used to date Angelica Rossi. She always planned to take over her grandparents' diner." His voice hit the cryogenic range.

"You don't want to see her again?"

"Do you want to see any of your exes again?"

I ran down the list (excepting Dianne, whom I see every day), wincing at some, smiling at others. "Call it a 50-50 chance. Angelica hasn't taken over the diner yet. She's working with her grandparents. She likes the early morning shift because she can bake without interruption."

"You talked to her? How is she?" Nick swallowed. "Would she want to see me again?"

Something else to wince at. "I don't think she would. Not a good ending?"

"No. She broke up with me right after ... I started living with you. I wasn't sure exactly why. She just screamed about how evil I was, that she couldn't be with anyone like me. Maybe because I was bi? But I never tried to hide it, and it wasn't like I cheated on her."

I flopped on my own bed and frowned at the ceiling. "Maybe she thought you did? People were always making stuff up and spreading it around. Belinda, my girlfriend at the time, was sure you and I were sleeping together. She's one of the never-agains."

"She must have been an idiot."

"She was. I decided I didn't need that kind of insanity in my life. Look, any flaming racist or homophobe would have stuck out in Lamar High. Most of West U went there, but Montrose and all points between did too. We were soaked in diversity. Unless Angelica thought you were cheating, I don't see why she flipped out. Did she just find out you were bi and thought it meant you always had other genders on the side?" I thought about her tense, disgusted expression as she said, "after I knew."

"I'll never know. It was just one more painful thing that didn't make sense. She was the last girl I dated. I thought men would be more reasonable." He pulled a frown. "Okay, I was wrong about that too."

"I just thought you realized you were more attracted to guys."

"That's mostly true. Sometimes a woman really knocks me out— like Dianne, for instance. Wow! Gorgeous and smart and sweet and anything else anybody could want. But I always talk myself out of trying. She's way out of my league."

I wanted to agree. But what if he was what she'd been waiting for and vice versa? I unclenched my jaw. "I don't know. Dianne has a few basic requirements, like speaking Spanish. Like her, you speak it natively."

"Sure, my mother's from Puerto Rico."

"That's fine. I—I've known her to date Anglos if they could carry on a conversation in Spanish, even with a bad accent."

He grinned. "Like yours."

Though Mother insisted I learn Spanish from my youngest days, I didn't have the gene to roll the Rs properly. Dianne's young cousins think it's hysterical to ask me to say *ferrocarril*. "Like mine. And she wants a partner who can dance. She moved from ballet to ballroom and folklórico, close to professional level."

"Well, your mother made me go to ballroom classes with you."

"You were pretty good, even though you were just starting. And Dianne doesn't mind teaching. She taught our whole house to dance, those who didn't know how already. Even Johnny."

"Hard to imagine. You've known her a while, then."

"Since the first week of college." I swallowed. I didn't want to get into details. "I'd like to see her happy. When we moved to Beauchamp, she kissed dating goodbye—more like booted it in the rear."

"Maybe she's asexual, which would be a shame."

"I ... really doubt it. Nor is she unreasonable, unlike Angelica. If she's mad at you, you'll know exactly why in at least two languages."

Nick chuckled, but his amusement died fast. "Angelica's why I didn't want to come to San Mateo. She worked here for her grandparents in the summers, and I knew she'd take over their restaurant someday. I can probably avoid her if I stay near the hospital. I won't go to the restaurant. It would be just my luck she'd come in to pick up her check while I'm there. But if you go back, you can pick up something for me." He scraped up the last bite of pie and then pointed to the nightstand. "I saved some for you. It's so good I can eat it without harking back to me trying to mow around the pecan tree and through the shells in our yard. Brett and Jessa never helped. Said they were allergic. Hah! Allergic to work, more like it."

"You'd bring bags of pecans to Scouts and trade them for tomatoes, squash, lemons, blackberries, whatever the other guys brought." I smiled, thinking of those days when our meeting room in the synagogue smelled like a farmer's market.

"And the synagogue staff would come take some for their food bank, they said. Who was the guy who got embarrassed because he never had anything until he raised pumpkins in senior year? Huge ones. He had so many he couldn't give them all away."

"That was Jacob. After everyone took enough for Halloween, Thanksgiving, and Christmas, he brought the rest to the senior center food bank and called it a service project. I got roped into helping him. Those suckers were heavy. It was a pumpkin-scented workout, especially when I dropped an armful." He rolled over and flicked off the light beside his bed. "Thanks for the walk down memory lane. Throw a bomb behind you as you leave."

I've often wished I could, at least for certain events. Our housekeeper from my childhood used to say she had a terrible memory. It wouldn't let her forget. Now I understood what she meant. I clicked off my light too and fell asleep to the rhythm of a snuffling Saint Bernard.

CHAPTER 19

My alarm nudged me out of bed forty-five minutes before I was due at Merry's bedside. That gave me time to shower, dress, and nab the last of the hotel's complimentary breakfast on my way to Merry's room.

Flowers from Merry's well-wishers adorned every surface. Their perfume saturated the air. I wondered who sent gardenias and how they found any in winter. Mother had planted gardenias along the front of the West U house, and Dianne always wore a gardenia perfume. The gardenia scent warred with the last of the Christmas greenery, shot with red berries and minuscule red ornaments.

Mrs. Ly rose when I entered the room and watched me take Merry's vitals. I needed coaching on blood pressure, not having done it before, but the rest went fine, and all the numbers were good. Mrs. Ly freshened up and went out to stalk breakfast in the hospital cafeteria.

Merry looked like a different person than she had the night before and not just because of the makeup her twin had artistically applied. "Is my face smeared? Zap's coming by after lunch."

"You look fine, a fresh-faced healthy girl-next-door."

She giggled. "I thought it was going to kill Cherry to put that look on me. She's bringing my own stuff later."

I pulled out my phone and started a video. The same song Johnny sang for Merry now filled the room as a viola solo. "Our intern sent a video this morning of Johnny, Godzilla, and the kittens."

She gazed at it in goofy awe, no doubt the result of kittens plus maternal hormones. "That's the song Johnny sang last night! Does he always sing for the cats?"

"Yes. It calms everybody down, including him, he says, and contributes to their healing. He moved the heated bed into the clinic where the mother cat can see them."

"I thought Godzilla was a male cat. He's nursing them!"

"No one seems to mind, even the mother cat. I think she's too injured to object to Godzilla."

"Weird. But he looks happy. Godzilla, I mean. Johnny looks happy too." She handed my phone back to me, just in time for a text to come through.

The wedding was postponed a day for medical reasons. I hoped Piano Man's brother would recover enough for his wedding. I glanced at the ceiling in a wordless, formless appeal. Sometimes I'm jealous of Dianne, whose religion has written prayers. Then there's the Sign of the Cross, a prayer in brief. I'm good with lyrics; improvisation, not as much. To my sister, I said, "Godzilla has always been weird. And Johnny's always happy when he can help an animal."

I looked up to see Dianne sweep into the room.

"I asked Dianne to do an Anointing of the Sick for me too," Merry said in a shy voice.

With a brief nod of welcome to me as I relocated to the window seat, Dianne arranged her scarf again and placed a bottle of water and a plastic cup of greenish-yellow oil on the side table.

She met my amused eyes. "The kitchen was open, and they gave me some olive oil. No more salad dressing." She assumed her priestly demeanor again. "Friends, we are gathered here ..."

I drifted away on Dianne's sonorous tones.

"Let us therefore commend our sister Meredith Arline to the grace and power of Christ ..." Dianne frowned. "I should commend you to your saint also, but you have no obvious saint's name. We'll take your nickname of Merry and use my saint, the Blessed Virgin Mary."

"I don't want to steal your saint," muttered Merry.

Dianne patted Merry's free hand. "It isn't official Church doctrine, but many Catholics call Mary the Mother of the World. I think that's the reason the Blessed Mother appears so many places—think of how many shrine names my mother had to choose from."

Mrs. Cortez, in her devotion to the Virgin Mary, named her children after shrines: Guadalupe, Lourdes, Zapopan, Fátima, Candelaria.

"Anyway," Dianne continued, "If she *is* Mother of the World, that explains why she shows up all over the globe. You cannot steal my saint, Merry. She is the mother of us all. You can also call on your own mother."

Merry looked eager. "Really? I can pray to my mother?"

"You can and you should. The Nicene Creed tells us all those who die in Christ are part of the communion of saints." Dianne's voice was as firm as when she gave tax advice, but much more tender. "Now let us anoint you with the sacramental oil and commend you to God's care."

She dipped the tips of her fingers into the olive oil and barely touched Merry's head, feet, and hands. She murmured prayers whose words I didn't always catch.

"You're tickling me." Merry gave a single, soft chuckle and wiggled her feet away.

After the Lord's Prayer, with Dianne ending it earlier than us Protestants, she announced, "Father in heaven, through this holy anointing grant Merry comfort in her suffering. When she is afraid, give her courage ..."

Merry's eyes closed. Dianne stepped back to let me sit by my sister again. I took her hand.

Her lips barely moved. "JD, I'm thirsty."

Even as close as she was, I had trouble hearing her. A glass of something stood on the tray by her bed. Not knowing how to work the bed, I raised her shoulders and sat behind her to prop her up.

Dianne covered her face. "Madre de Dios, JD. You just showed me a gender-swapped pietà."

The Virgin Mary holding her crucified Son? I didn't care for that image.

I held the glass to Merry's cracked, dry lips. She let me hold it but guided it to drink deep. Her now-moist lips relaxed into a flicker of a smile as I eased her back down and she drifted into slumber.

Mrs. Ly returned to relieve me at the end of my shift. Suddenly exhausted, I returned to the hotel and laid down for the first good sleep I'd had in days. A text from Dianne in the late afternoon woke me.

Everyone, she said, had been snacking on bits of this and that since the day before and was ready for a real meal. She suggested the place next door to the hotel, Boudreaux's Italian Garden.

I frowned, trying to parse the name with the declared cuisine. Cajun-Italian fusion? The possibility of pasta seasoned with Zatarain's crab boil seemed tame in comparison to my recent adventures. I yawned and set myself in motion.

Boudreaux's Christmas tree, still crisp, took up a third of the reception area. It flashed its lights proudly over a nest of unopened presents.

"We're keeping it up through Epiphany." The hostess, perky as her tree, looked like Christmas was still fun for her, however long it continued. "We're offering a different dessert for each of the twelve days of Christmas, with Kings' Cake on January 6. Are you with the service dog? He's adorable."

I've spent a good part of my adult life saying, "I'm with the band." Now the band had been upstaged, and I'd be saying, "I'm with the dog."

She led me to Saint's table, on the far side of the restaurant, out of traffic, where he could look out the window. Not that he'd do that while on duty. Pressing next to Nick's leg, he chowed down on chicken, compliments of the chef. I hoped we'd get service as good.

I greeted Dianne, Nick—and Johnny? His presence surprised me.

"Chantal showed up to spend a few days with Godzilla before her New Year's gig. She'll help Darryl with the cats until I get back." Johnny held up his phone to show us a photo of our other housemate and soprano-bandleader Chantal with a lap full of kittens.

Godzilla stood on his hind legs, his forelegs in her lap, another kitten in his mouth. Everyone made appropriate noises for precious kittens.

Johnny continued, "I came to take my grandmother back to Beauchamp. At Gregg House she'll be close by if Merry takes a turn for the worse. I'll sit with Merry after dinner."

Nick dropped his hand on Saint's head. "I think we should keep our shifts going through tonight at least." He consulted his phone. "I'll go in at 9:00. Can you do midnight, JD? Zap's probably up for the 3:00 AM shift."

I nodded and cut a slice of bread from the communal loaf.

Dianne beckoned a server. "How about a bottle of wine to split? We all need it after the last day. We'll toast Merry and the baby."

Nick shook his head. "None for me, thanks, but feel free."

I perked up. That would leave more for the rest of us.

Johnny dipped his bread in the olive oil. "JD, did you hear any more from Jessa? I've been doing research, and I wanted to ask about her parents' symptoms, particularly whether they experienced abdominal issues or leg cramps."

"They did." I scrolled through Jessa's texts. "Wait, no. That was Angelica's grandparents. I don't see anything about symptoms from Jessa." I glanced at Nick. "I could ask."

"If you dare say anything about me—" he scowled.

"I won't. I'm sure I haven't the slightest idea where you are, but I can make friendly, concerned conversation."

He snorted and tore off a piece of bread.

The bread really was great. The server brought us another loaf.

I started carving slices. "What do you suspect, Johnny?"

"I don't have enough data."

I eyed him. "You never do. What's your best guess? Speculation, I mean."

Johnny looked nauseous, like he always does when asked to guess. "If I saw a body that looked like the elder Thorntons and discovered they'd had symptoms like Angelica's grandparents, I'd suspect arsenic poisoning. But Angelica's family has nothing to do with the Thorntons."

The bread sank in my stomach like a limestone boulder. I took a big gulp of the wine Dianne poured for me. I told myself to slow down. I wanted to talk to keep myself from drinking, but I said nothing. I did not want to tell Nick in public that his high-school girlfriend was now his sister-in-law. Anyway, I couldn't see a connection to arsenic.

Nick tore off another piece of bread. "In my studies, ingesting arsenic meant you were dead."

"That would depend on how much," Johnny replied, busy with his own bread. "If they ingested the same small amount over time, it's not surprising that the smaller person died and the larger didn't. I don't think it was a one-time dose. Spots don't appear right away."

"Look, Johnny." Nick crunched the bread with a ferocious gnashing of his teeth. "We've got two equally unpleasant subjects here, both unsuitable for the dinner table: bodily functions and my so-called family. If you want to play pathologist, fine, but I don't want to hear about it."

The server brought our plates at that point, breaking off the conversation (or in Johnny's case, lecture).

My mind kept spinning throughout the delicious dinner. We passed around our plates to give everyone got a sample of lasagna, grilled plum and pancetta panzanella salad, chicken frittata, and Caprese salad. I accepted another glass of wine from Dianne, since she was having seconds too.

Dianne and Johnny have promised/threatened to throw me out of the house if I get drunk and incapacitated again. I may have done so a few times in the past, like whenever I'm under stress. My current personal rule is that I have one drink when other people are drinking, but I felt I could stretch it to two glasses of wine. After the last few days, I deserved it.

We shared our desserts too—gelato (the special of this day of Christmas), Concord grape granita (despite the cold), panna cotta, and rainbow almond cookies. I kidnapped the wine bottle from Dianne and poured the dregs into my glass. Dianne swirled the last of her gelato around her mouth with a reverence most people save for Communion. Half a glass of wine stood by her elbow.

"Are you going to drink that?" I asked.

CHAPTER 20

Merry slept through the rest of my shift, except for when the hospital nurse woke her up for something, probably to give her a sleeping pill with a tall glass of grape juice. She was supposed to drink lots to help her milk come in. She gulped it and grumbled herself back to sleep.

Watching her monitors bored me almost to sleep. No changes were great, but I had trouble keeping my eyes open.

Several times I walked over to the NICU to watch Baby Jade. Sound didn't travel through the window, and the silent movements looked like a slow ballet for nurses and machinery. The babies, of course, lay still, but for their little chests rising and falling, hard to see. Once I called through the intercom for a report to give Merry; the baby was fine, making progress. That comforted me, putting to rest the terror I hadn't wanted to speak out loud.

When I escaped outdoors, the cold wind snapping at my face woke me right up. I wasn't ready to sleep but I didn't want to wake Nick while I puttered around the room. I coaxed my car into starting and drove around town, lying still in the early morning hours. I found myself headed toward Gina's and more of Angelica's cobbler. Maybe without ice cream this time, unless the coffee warmed me up.

Once again, I stepped into a timeless past when I opened the restaurant door. Angelica seemed glad to see me. At my request, she brought a duplicate of my previous order. Why mess with success?

She gestured to a gift basket by the Christmas tree. "I was hoping you'd come back. I put together a basket for your sister with pink and green baby clothes, for Jade. I guess that's what y'all are calling her?"

I examined the rolls of socks, bibs, and blankets among the tins of cookies and candies and baby products. "Jadey, actually."

"What?" Angelica laughed but looked puzzled. "Like JD?"

I laughed too, embarrassed. "Merry wanted to name her baby after me, in addition to her mother and grandmother, and came up with Jadey. That sounds better than JDette or JDrine, the other Southern fallbacks to feminize names, don't you think?"

She kept chuckling as she served my food.

I'd reveled in half the cobbler when three people stumbled through the door. They sounded like a crowd of ten at a UT football game or an audience of a lowest-common-denominator comic, since they were laughing so hard.

I frowned at the interruption of my silent time travel and cobbler worship.

Angelica ran out of the kitchen. I started to rise, intending to back her up and enforce her decrees, if necessary. Her first words made me sit down again.

"Brett! Keep it down. Please!" She used both hands to reach inside his coat and latch onto his shirt.

"No worries, Angie-baby!" he caroled, this grown-up (or at least older) version of Nick's younger stepbrother, unofficially voted Most Punchable Face in high school. "We'll just pick up a bottle of wine and leave. Make it two."

"You promised us breakfast," objected one of his companions, who were identically dressed in jeans and short black fleece coats. They wore different blue shirts (striped, plaid, solid). This guy wore plaid.

"Yeah," said Stripes.

"Brett, I can't serve wine after 2:00 a.m." Angelica's voice was strung tight like a piano string.

"You're not serving it. I'm taking it."

"Granddad said you have to quit raiding the inventory. Sit down and I'll make you all breakfast." She encouraged him in my direction with a bright smile. "Look who's here! JD Thompson, from high school. Remember?"

I waved a hand. "Go, Native Americans."

Brett (solid blue shirt) and his satellites ambled toward my booth. "That's *Indians*. I don't care what they say now."

"I think I heard they changed the mascot to Texans, but whatever." I tried to guess what they were high or strung out on. Alcohol, I could smell. A faint aroma of weed. Eyes dilated, staggering gait, slurred speech.

Brett and Stripes squashed into the seat across from me, leaving Plaid, disconsolate, to join me, leaving as much room between us as possible. With a tense smile, Angelica plunked down three mugs of steaming black coffee in front of them.

"Sorry for the loss of your mother," I said, for lack of anything else to say.

His face screwed up as he tried to hold back tears. "My mother! She died of diabetes because she wouldn't give up her sweets. Always with the sugar. Angelica and I took her sugar-free desserts every Sunday. She'd eat one serving in front of me and then go for the sweet dessert we brought my dad behind my back, I found out later. She could have lived to be a hundred!"

"That's rough," I agreed, for something to say.

Brett stared at me. "I know you from somewhere."

"Lamar High School." I stirred my coffee.

"Twenty-five hundred people there. Gotta narrow it down."

"Second trombone in orchestra with Angelica."

"That wasn't it. I wasn't into music. Didn't go to any concerts until I started dating Angelica at the end of junior year."

My eyes cut over to the grill, where bacon sizzled. Angelica flipped pancakes and stirred scrambled eggs. Since she seemed occupied, I dared to say, "I was in Scouts with your stepbrother Nick. I used to come over to your house to work on projects."

Brett grinned, gleeful, straight out of a horror movie.

Stripes guffawed and nudged Brett. "Tell him what you told us about your stepbrother."

"Nah, man." But he looked like he couldn't wait to tell.

"Yeah, tell it. It's hysterical," Plaid chimed in.

Brett glanced at Angelica, now working on hashbrowns. He leaned forward and whispered. "My mother married his father when I was starting high school, and I hated Nick's guts. We had to share a room, because the house only had three bedrooms. He said he was bi-sex-u-al."

"Queer."

"Fag."

"And I couldn't stand that. But even so, his dad and grandfather thought he walked on water, little Mr. Boy Scout. Then he started dating Angie, and I really couldn't stand that. So one day I went to his dad, crying, and said Nick tried to rape me. His dad was so mad, he threw Nick out of the house right then and there. Angie was there too, and she broke up with him on the spot and never spoke to him again. Of course, she was very, very, *very* sympathetic to me. I let her comfort me." He guffawed and pounded the table. His friends joined in, though they'd heard the story before.

He wiped his eyes. "It gets better. His grandfather was going to send him to college, give him a place in the family firm, but of course he wasn't going to do that for any pedo, so he paid for Nick to go somewhere else and cut him out of the will. He left everything to Nick's dad. Gramps died a year later, and Nick's dad adopted me and my sister, making us next in line for the inheritance, and man, he's loaded. I'll be set for life, even after splitting it with my sister, never mind what Angie will get from her family."

I froze, willing myself not to react. I hope quantum theory is true, the one that says every possibility happens in duplicate universes. I enjoyed the one where I grabbed Brett by his shirt and punched him with enough force to shatter his nose. And his friends? In payment for the names they called Nick, I gave them each a big old kiss on the lips. Sadly none of that happened in this universe, where I had too much to lose.

A noise made me raise my eyes. Angelica stood behind him with three plates of food, in danger of flying out of her shaking hands.

She dropped them on the table beside ours and fled back to the kitchen.

"Awesome, amirite?" chortled Stripes. "Got rid of the stepbrother, got his girlfriend, got all the bennies of the first-born son."

Plaid punched my arm while laughing. "Just super. Brett's a genius."

"Amazing," I said in flat tones. "The family just believed you? They didn't take you to the ER?"

Brett made a sad-eyed puppy face. "I begged them not to. Said it would retraumatize me. Said the same thing about therapy. Dad said he was always afraid Nick would do something like this, but his first wife, the slut who ran away, encouraged him to have faith in their boy. I gave them enough details they believed me, and I said I'd managed to fight my way free before anything *really* happened, you know?" His face morphed into pure evil.

I had a suspicion how he'd acquired those realistic details. I was going to be mad if I threw up that divine cobbler, but my stomach was making threats, churning hard enough for me to imagine bacon and eggs tumbling and commingling.

I stood up and shoved Plaid out of the booth. I looked at the watch I did not have because I always check my phone instead. "Look at the time. I've got to get going. And here's your breakfast." When I escaped the booth, I served them the plates Angelica had left. It didn't seem to occur to them that she might have overheard. I didn't see her anywhere.

They were still laughing when I walked away. I pushed open the kitchen door and saw her crying into her phone. On the kitchen island in front of her, a blender whirred, approaching take-off velocity.

I raised my voice over the blender. "I need to pay you, and I'll take the two cobblers, if you've got them ready."

"Hang on, Jessa." She wiped her running nose with one hand and waved at the Styrofoam cube boxes in a bag with the other. "Just take them. And the basket. Go."

I picked up the boxes. "Can I do anything for you? I don't want to leave you like this."

Her voice choked back a scream. "What can anybody do? Just get out." She jumped up and pounded the Off button on the blender.

I pulled my business card from my pocket and laid it on the corner of the kitchen island. "If you think of anything later, let me know— rides to anywhere, help moving, legal services, even just a listening ear." I thought about mentioning Nick, but decided the situation was complicated enough. Surely she'd remember that I was his friend.

Looking at her face turning even redder, with more tears and snot coursing to her chin, I turned on my heel and obeyed her command, grasping Merry's basket and juggling it with the cobblers.

I didn't look at Brett and his posse. They had already forgotten about me. Their sneers about what they'd done to some other soul followed me out the door.

CHAPTER 21

’d like to say I drove five miles under the speed limit because I was impaired after what I heard. The truth is I just didn’t want to face Nick. I hadn’t told him his stepbrother had married his old girlfriend. That didn’t affect his life then or now. But his stepbrother’s confession—boast—cleared up many questions while making the situation worse. Brett lied. The family believed him.

My mind still thrumming like Angelica’s blender, I tiptoed into the hotel room in hopes Nick wouldn’t wake up. But the hotel door clicked in that specially designed way to make as much noise as possible, and Nick sat up in bed and flicked on the light beside his bed. Saint just raised his head.

“Sorry, man.” I scrambled for something to say. “I brought your cobbler. I’ll put it in the fridge.”

He rubbed his face. “No problem. I was half awake. I’m usually up at this time. I’ll call the cobbler breakfast and take Saint for a good long walk.”

I glanced at the window, though the blackout curtains were drawn. Dark would reign for another couple of hours.

Nick flashed his twisted smile. “In the dark, we don’t have to deal with anyone, and they don’t mess with us.”

I believed that. No one would bother a guy that tall or his giant dog.

Both Nick's voice and demeanor changed. "Are you okay, JD?"

I handed him one of the Styrofoam boxes and a plastic fork. I poured water into the coffeemaker, which grumbled its way into function. Setting the other cobbler box on the desk, I turned the desk chair around and straddled it backwards to give me someplace to rest my arms. "Not really, but that's because I have to tell you something. I don't know when's the best time, so I'm going with the sooner, the better."

Nick stopped with the fork halfway to his mouth. He stared at the shiny, deep purple berries and let the fork drift back down. He gestured to Saint, who came over and laid his head in Nick's lap. "Go on."

"Did you know Brett married Angelica?"

Nick's face flamed in fury. Saint licked Nick's shaking hand. "No."

I inhaled, hoping and failing to find courage. I hated to deliver bad news to my clients. Not every case ends with multimillion dollar judgments or even a client's minimal desires—most don't—but it's worse when I have to give bad news to a friend. I took a deep breath and repeated what Brett said, but in a flat voice with none of his bragging and gloating.

Nick's face bleached paler than mine. His hands shook except when Saint nudged him. Then Nick ran his hands through the rough Saint Bernard coat and murmured things like, "It's okay, boy. Everything's fine. It will be. I promise."

I didn't point out that Saint wasn't the one worried.

When I ran out of words, silence lay between us as wide as the Rio Grande.

Nick stood up. "Let's go walkies, Saint."

I mirrored him. "I'll go with you."

"Don't."

"You shouldn't go alone."

"I won't. Saint will be with me." He snatched Saint's leash from the desk. He avoided my eyes. "I don't want any other company. I'm going to call a friend."

And I was chopped liver? "I'll leave and you can have the room."

"I need to move!" he shouted.

We both winced and froze as we listened for complaints from other guests. He snapped the leash on Saint and marched out.

The door clicked behind him, still too loud. Seconds later, the elevator dinged to announce its arrival. When the heavy doors clanked open, I launched into action. Action consisted of intense pacing in the room's limited space, but it counted as something.

After the tenth lap, I pulled back the curtains to squint into the darkness, broken only by the foggy streetlights. I didn't see Nick and Saint. I traipsed back and forth some more. I tried the breathing technique Nick taught Merry in the car. I told myself Saint would stay by Nick's side and bring him home.

A soft whining and scratching at the door interrupted my scattered thoughts. I threw the door open to gaze into Saint's deep brown eyes, pleading. I looked up and down the hall. No Nick.

My brain clicked on. An unaccompanied service dog meant I had to follow him.

I checked my pocket for my keycard and dashed out the door. Before the door slammed shut, other thoughts demanded attention. I stepped back in the room and breathed deep.

Nick could be in shock. I grabbed a bottle of water and a folded blanket from the closet.

Did he need medicine? What kind? I stepped in the bathroom and seized his dopp kit. Would that have everything he needed, whatever it was? I found his backpack in one of the dresser drawers. Saint whined and took my hand in his mouth. Dang, I'm glad he didn't bite down with those chompers.

"We'll go in a minute, boy, but I'm useless on my own." After I pitched in the water bottle and dopp kit, I slung the backpack over my shoulder. I fumbled with the extra straps on Saint's harness. Because they seemed to be for the purpose of making him a pack animal, I used them to secure the blanket to his back. I opened the door, and Saint galloped toward the elevator.

I glanced around the room for anything else we needed. I picked up my coat—and then removed the backpack, put on the coat, and picked up the backpack again. I met Saint on my way to the elevator, and he tugged me along, determined not to lose me again.

He stood on his hind legs and pressed the elevator button.

His skill impressed me, though to be honest, he couldn't go wrong in a two-story hotel. "Good boy!"

When we hit the lobby, the desk clerk, a red-haired youngster who might have graduated high school last week, shouted, "That dog's not supposed to be in here. I tried to shoo him away, and he ran to the elevators."

"Service dog," I panted as Saint picked up the pace.

"I called Animal Control and left a message. They're not open at night. I called my manager. He'll be here any minute."

I paused to let the entrance doors pull back. I didn't remember them being this slow. Also impatient, Saint danced in front of them. "Tell him that instead of suing his corporate pants off, I'll offer a training special for his employees on service dogs. Here's a free sample. When a service dog by himself approaches you, follow him. He's trying to find help for his handler."

"I'm not going near that monster!" the kid shouted after me. "Besides, I can't leave the desk."

I think that's what he said. I had to run after Saint, who shot out of the building like a bullet when the doors opened. I couldn't keep up with him. I told myself I didn't want to run full out in the dark over unfamiliar territory. I told him the same thing when he stopped at the end of the building and turned back at me in disgust. As I got closer, he took off again, around the side.

I panicked when he turned around another corner to the backside of the hotel. I forced my legs to go faster. Saint came to a sudden stop and lay beside a still, dark form on the ground.

CHAPTER 22

I ran forward with a burst of new energy. "Nick!"

At first I thought I heard Nick speaking. Then I saw his phone a foot away, lit up.

The voice on the call—an older Latine, sex undetermined, but the tone and accent providing clues about the rest—rivaled me for panic. "Nick! Nick! Can you speak! I've called the ambulance. They'll be there in a minute. Are you okay!"

I picked up the phone. "I'm Nick's friend. Saint fetched me. I brought all his stuff, but I don't know what to do with it."

"Thank God! I don't know either, or even where he is. He said, 'Saint says I'm having a seizure' and stopped talking. I heard Saint bark. I called an ambulance. I told them to triangulate with Nick's phone, but I don't know if they did."

Sounds came out of Nick's mouth that sounded like "No ambulance." Saint nestled closer and licked the back of Nick's hand.

Seeing Saint's leash on the ground, I picked it up. Had Nick turned him loose to find help? "We're across the street from a hospital, and we've got a nurse in our group. We'll get care for him right away."

"Let me know how he's doing later, okay?"

"Sure. Can you try to call off the ambulance?"

They agreed and cut the connection. I pulled out my own phone and knelt beside Nick, huddled in a fetal position.

"M kay," he muttered in slurred words.

"You don't look okay. What's wrong?"

He swallowed. "Seezhr."

"I brought your stuff. What do you need?" I removed the blanket from Saint's back and covered them both with it.

"Don't. Need. Anything. Z'over." He struggled to sit up, but his limbs flopped, uncontrolled. His body was still on strike.

I commanded, "This one I know. Lie still until someone checks you out. You might have hit your head or broken a bone."

He gave a deep, long sigh that turned into a groan. He slammed his lips together in what looked like frustration and curled up tighter on the ground. Saint snuffled in and licked his hand harder.

I rummaged through his gear. "Here's something. Lorazepam."

"No. Too late. Shut up, JD." Nick tried again and rolled himself into a cross-legged position. He held his head in his hands like the world's heaviest bowling ball. Saint still found his hand to lick.

"I'll ask Mrs. Ly or Johnny to help."

Nick took a deep breath and put it all behind the one word. "No!"

Saint and I both stared at him.

He took several more breaths before continuing in a near-normal voice. "Yes, I had a seizure. My stupid, stupid brain." Nick put his arms around Saint's neck and hugged him. "Saint knew before I did. He's brilliant that way."

I eyed Saint with respect. "He's brilliant, yeah."

Saint licked Nick's ear. Nick chuckled. "Okay, boy, that's enough. He nudged me toward the grass and let me collapse on him to break my fall. So I didn't hit my head or break anything. He barked to raise the alarm. He pushed me over on my side and barked again. When no one came, he went to get help. You, apparently."

"He went to the desk clerk first, but the idiot didn't know the protocol. He called Animal Control and his manager."

Nick groaned. Saint went back to licking Nick's hand.

"Don't worry. Send them to me if they give you any grief. Saint read the room and recognized that guy as Useless Man. Saint punched the elevator button and scratched at the door."

"I had either a focal onset aware seizure or a myoclonic seizure. It felt like both, if that's possible."

I opened the water bottle and handed it to him. When he fumbled, I helped guide it to his mouth for a long drink.

"I don't think I lost consciousness. Maybe I did." He let me take the bottle away. He punctuated each sentence with several breaths. "It was over before you arrived. It's too late for meds to do anything. It takes a while to recover." He let loose a string of four-letter words, like a tongue-twister. A grin flickered. "If I can say that whole thing, I'm just about recovered."

He'd answered almost all my questions. "Why is Saint licking your hand?"

Nick patted the dog's head with the unlicked hand. "He's licking the Shen Men point."

"That sounds like acupuncture." I'd heard a lot about acupuncture. Johnny uses it on his cat clients.

"It is. The practitioner said rubbing that point might help me recover faster. I trained Saint to lick it. It feels nice and calms me down." He held out his hand and bent his other wrist. Saint moved to that one. Nick sighed again. "I haven't had a seizure for seven months. I hoped I was cured. Now I'll have to wait three months before I can drive again."

"If you can go seven months, you must be getting better."

"Anybody ever tell you you're a pain?" He sounded despondent.

"Pretty much always. Would you humor me and go to the hospital —" I held up my hands to ward off his angry expression. "Just the cafeteria. I had breakfast, but you didn't. If you get through a meal without incident, I'll accept that you're recovered."

He thought about it. "I'll go you one better. I'll go to a meeting in the hospital after breakfast. Will that make you happy, that I'm in a hospital for some time where care is available? I'll visit Merry afterwards."

Meeting? How did he know anyone to meet with in San Mateo? Maybe he'd found some kind of skills review, serendipitously offered when he was in town.

My curiosity must have shown in my face, because he said, "It's a networking function. Most towns have it. Friends of Bill W."

Bill must have a lot of friends. "Good that you're networking already." I scrambled to my feet and held out a hand to Nick.

He held on with something less than dead weight and got to his feet. Saint pressed against his legs, making him steadier. "You don't have to help me up. Saint's trained to do that. He'll feel like he failed to do his job."

"Sorry, Saint. I'll do better next time."

Nick's laugh was more of a cackle.

CHAPTER 23

We parted after an uneventful breakfast. Nick's gait now had only the barest hint of a limp. Saint stayed close by, ready for anything.

My phone chirped with a message from our new piano-playing friend. His brother's wedding would take place in the chapel at 2:00, without fail. Could Dianne and I still play and sing for it? I checked with Dianne and confirmed.

I then went to Merry's room to hear the news of the day. The doctor wanted her in the hospital until they were sure she'd recovered from maternal chorio—I'm lost. Suffice to say, she needed treatment, and Baby Jade needed time to mature. She'd be in NICU for weeks yet.

With Mrs. Ly declaring our intense medical watches over and Merry planning to spend the majority of her time in the nursery, our old gang broke up. My father wanted to go back to Houston because "he had work to do," his excuse for bailing out of everything ever. Mallory straightened her slumped shoulders and gave us all an apologetic smile as she followed him out of the room.

At least one person would stay in San Mateo with Merry each day, but we'd make Gregg House our base of operations. Cherry would drive home to Waco; she had a New Year's Eve date. When she recovered from that, she'd come to Beauchamp to collect our grandparents.

I sent Nick a text about the plans. I walked back to the hotel with no fixed idea of what to do. Lying in bed staring at the ceiling sounded good. When I got bored with that, I'd turn over and stare at the wall until time to go to the wedding.

My phone rang before I put this ambitious plan into action.

The screen told me Unknown Caller. I thought the high-pitched voice was female, but I couldn't make out her garbled words. After a few seconds, having heard "Nick," "Brett," and "Angelica," I hazarded a guess. "Jessa?" I tried not to roll my eyes at yet one more interruption from Nick's bratty sister.

"Yes," Jessa sobbed. "Angelica called me ..."

Fortunately I'd heard the story already, because Nick's sister wept through it. Her gist was they had to find Nick right away, make it up to him, that their gravely ill father wanted to beg Nick's forgiveness before he died.

I could and did honestly say that I didn't know Nick's location. "I'm not saying I won't search for him but don't count on anything. He might not want to see his father. After all, no one ever asked Nick if Brett's accusations were true."

"I told them they should ask him!" She dissolved into hiccupping sobs again. "Where could he be?"

Guilt and compassion warred within me. Jessa had been a young teen when all this started, annoying but not totally mean, from what I remembered. I couldn't betray Nick, though. I weaseled off the call. "There's no telling. I'll let you know if I learn anything."

I had just enough time to meet Dianne in the cafeteria and gulp some water before seeking out the chapel for the wedding. She wore her maroon sweater dress, but she'd wound the scarf around her neck and tied it in a perky way. Just like that, it shed its appearance as a vestment.

We went over our set. We hummed a brief rehearsal on our way down the hall. The words weren't new, just who was singing them when.

I followed her into the chapel and ran into her when she stopped short and caught her breath.

Only slightly larger than the legal limits to swing a medium-sized cat, the room held no more than twenty people. It still gave off the energy of a cathedral-sized wedding, the kind Dianne's family throws.

The couple stood by the keyboard we'd kidnapped with the musician we'd met at Jadey's baptism. I barely recognized him with his hair slicked down and his long-sleeved polo and chinos. He gave me a grin and a thumbs-up. I did the same, aiming towards him and the small silver cross on the small wooden table doubling as an altar. I might have mouthed, "Thanks."

In daylight, the room was bright and welcoming. Behind the altar stood a floor-to-ceiling stained-glass window of religiously neutral flowers and vines in bright shades of blue and green. Tall windows on either side shone light on the altar. Icons and pictures from other religions lined the walls, doing their best to welcome everyone.

The slim Asian bride rocked a simple but dramatic long lace gown, her veil draped over her face. Her husband-to-be was so thin his black suit seemed empty. His hands were mottled with bruises, his face gaunt and drawn. He seemed to be of mixed race, maybe Black and Asian, but with a gray, sickly skin color.

Staring at the groom, Dianne breathed the words, audible only to me. "Wow. That guy's got angel eyes."

"Angel eyes?"

She zoomed toward the group gathered at the piano but whispered over her shoulder, "Like Nick."

The groom did have deep brown expressive eyes, currently excited with an underlay of suffering, the kind of eyes a person could drown in. That was angel eyes? And Nick had them? Dianne had noticed? That hurt.

After performing a few dance steps with them, she returned and guided me to seats near the piano. She whispered, "Okay, we'll sing 'I've Been Waiting for You' as an intro. Right after the vows, a happy version of 'Angel Eyes.' As the outro and first dance, 'Andante, Andante,' more like an adagio because he has to lean on his walker."

"You're getting this happy version of 'Angel Eyes' where?"

"From my fevered brain. Shut up and let me write." She scribbled on the wedding program. "Can you transpose it down a step for me?"

"Of course."

After the bride and groom joined hands and the officiant nodded, we barreled into "I've Been Waiting for You." Dianne not only sang the first verse; she acted it, turning to me with her own angel eyes and smiling earnestly as she sang to me about those old feelings.

Similar feelings overwhelmed me, not just from our history. I'd first sung this song as a duet to Mallory, back when I hoped we'd be a thing, before she fell for my dad. Now I could barely rasp my verse out. Looking concerned, Dianne held back in our harmony section. Somewhere I managed a deep breath and urged her into a crescendo so we could both belt out "I've Been Waiting for You." I did better on the next verse and finished strong.

We set the tone for the whole ceremony. Nobody that I could see made it through without tears. Instead of a lying deceiver with beautiful eyes, Dianne sang about the most wonderful man in the world with beautiful eyes. People liked it.

The bride and groom gazed rapturously into each other's eyes, their smiles full of public love and intimate secrets. They leaned hard into each other with a minimum of gliding steps as Dianne brought the house down with "Andante, Andante" as slow as it's possible to sing it, though still with a lilting roll.

I helped push the piano to the cafeteria, following the wedding guests. After the bride and groom cut the towering cake, the original pianist whispered to Dianne, who told me to play "Kisses of Fire" and get everybody on the dance floor. I did, and he and she romped around the room, pulling in the wedding guests and then anybody who wandered into the cafeteria.

Dianne's been pulling partygoers to their feet since she did the Macarena at age five at her party-planner mother's events. She's only gotten better, and even the kitchen workers were rocking out by my sixth trip through the song.

She didn't exempt Nick when he walked in with Saint by his side. The tragedy still heavy on his face turned into bemusement as Dianne roped him into the scene.

Nick could dance, and, it turned out, Saint could too. At a

command from Nick, he rose on his hind legs and pawed the air in front of Dianne. He stood tall enough to look into her eyes, and cameras flashed around the room at the dog-and-girl dance.

CHAPTER 24

Nick hung around until we'd finished playing and wished the couple well (and asked for someone to send me the video of Saint and Dianne dancing). Dianne's farewells lasted longer than mine, and Nick pulled me aside.

"Since we're off medical duty, would it be possible to go to Houston tomorrow? I could pick up my stuff at your dad's house." Nick didn't meet my eyes. "I think I should go see my father. I don't much care what he has to say, and I'm not ready to forgive him. But at the baptism the other night, I claimed to know something about God. My conduct ought to show it."

I frowned. "Lots of opinions on what that looks like. You could consult a spiritual advisor. Johnny's deep in his Jewish studies, and Dianne could declare another emergency to don her priestly role."

"I have my own spiritual advisors."

"And they say to go see your father?" I failed to banish skepticism from my voice.

"No, they said to guard my own mental health. I decided to listen to my own soul. It tells me I can put myself aside for a few minutes and make a man's passing easier. I'd want someone to do the same for me." An evil smile flashed across his face. "I'll try to resist the temptation to rub his face in his choice of a son when he wouldn't even listen to me."

"You could. I'm also thinking of your hard-won peace of mind over the years. Do you owe it to the guy who abandoned you to disturb that peace?"

"My peace, as you call it, has already been severely disturbed. I'll do this thing on the theory that I won't let his actions define mine. Also, I scheduled a remote appointment with my therapist for right afterwards."

"That will make it better. I can take you to your favorite bar too."

He shook his head and laughed. "Not necessary."

"And you could, while you're with him, try to get samples for arsenic testing."

Nick shook his head again, but with a different vibe. "Absolutely not. It's none of my business. Besides, wouldn't it be awkward to ask for hair and fingernail samples?"

He had a point.

Since we'd missed the hotel checkout time, we decided to stay overnight and set out for Houston early in the morning. Nick said he'd rent another trailer for us—Johnny had returned the one we had, but I thought we could borrow Johnny's truck.

Nick followed me to the backyard shelter, also carrying a tray of cat cuisine. Saint came too, to do his business and run around the backyard. I'm glad Nick realized the cats weren't ready to meet a Saint Bernard, no matter how friendly.

We entered the vast old barn, now converted to a luxury catitat. I nodded in the direction of Johnny's truck, brought inside for the cold snap. I continued toward the cat condos, where dozens of felines practiced for their singing and dancing auditions. They slinked sinuously, howling in multipart non-harmony.

Nick caught up to me a minute later and began serving the cats. "Is that truck old enough to drink? Looks like it's been on a few benders."

Like our neighboring farmers and ranchers, Johnny needed a good working truck. These folks defined such a truck as one that ran until all the children of the house were grown. He'd bought this truck second or third hand. The scorching Texas sun had long ago faded the original bright red right off the color chart; however, the engine was in good shape.

Exterior and interior, not so much. A household debate raged about the last owner. I voted for a cougar, Dianne for a bear, and Chantal, an alligator. Something with immense, long claws, we agreed. Our intern thought all three had thrown a party on the standard cab's bench seat. A replacement seat sat in the corner of the barn. Because it arrived just before the holiday hoopla started, I expected it would sit there some time. Johnny thought throwing a blanket over the shredded seat was an adequate stopgap fix.

"It's at least old enough to vote." I jerked my hand back as a calico cat took a swipe literally at the hand that fed her. "But it runs, and we have a livestock trailer that's hauled a jaguar. Between that and the covered truck bed, we should be able to haul the rest of your things. We've got hauling down to, if not a science, at least a solid conspiracy theory."

Nick wrinkled his nose. "What if I don't want my belongings to smell like jaguar poop?"

"No danger of that. We wash it every time we use it, and we have tarps to line the inside, for non-fauna loads."

Nick ran out of excuses, though he thought of a few more as we sped down the road toward Houston. Owners considered shocks even less necessary than a bench seat.

When we arrived at the Thompson house, we unhitched the trailer. From there, Nick had to guide me to his father's house. His family no longer lived in the little bungalow where he'd grown up. Brett and Angelica had lived in it before they moved to San Mateo. Their father and Jessa now lived in the bigger house inherited from Nick's grandfather on Wesleyan Street.

I asked if he wanted my support as well as Saint's, but he thought he could handle a fifteen-minute visit without melting.

He frowned for emphasis. "Fifteen minutes. Got it?"

"Got it. I'll go get gas and sodas."

"Dr. Pepper for me. And an orange cupcake, to reward me for my courage."

"Agreed."

We both twitched when I pulled into his father's driveway. I expected an older, dignified house like where I grew up, not a modern monstrosity from a crack-snorting architect's nightmares. West U began demolishing its historical houses during my childhood. Usually people built fake historical replacements to fit in with the neighborhood vibe. Nick's parents ... hadn't.

"That's not how Grandpa's house looked," muttered Nick. "I changed my mind. Would you come in with me?"

"Sure, I understand. The spaceship might take off before I could get back to you."

CHAPTER 25

From the front, I couldn't determine the house's overall shape. It seemed like an exercise in avoiding right angles, though not angles in general. The grim, dark, deeply hooded roof squatted over a dark base. The glowing clerestory windows bisecting the middle gave it a spaceship look. Maybe the house was an example of statement architecture, a statement full of four-letter words.

Jessa admitted us. I could still trace the bouncy, annoying, ginger-haired teen through the outer husk of the worried, grieving twenty-five-year-old woman. We sorted ourselves. Nick would go to his father's room with Saint, and I would remain with Jessa.

She zoomed up the curved staircase, as malformed as the rest of the house, to deposit Nick with his father. I remained in the living room and gawked at the random, unidentifiable blocks of stone that, by their display, proclaimed themselves as art. I didn't buy it.

Jessa made another trip upstairs with refreshments. Running those stairs would keep a person in shape. She sped through the kitchen one last time to gather food and drink for me.

She plunked down a slice of pie and a cup of coffee on the asymmetrical coffee table in front of me. "I hope you don't mind sugar-free pie. When Brett and Angelica lived nearby, they always brought desserts for Sunday dinner. Angelica would bake a sugar-free dessert for Mom, who was diabetic, in addition to a sweet one for Dad. I just gave him the last sweet piece."

I picked up the plate. "Nice of her."

Jessa forced a smile. "Yes, but Mom only ate the sugar-free version in front of Angelica and Brett. Then she'd eat Dad's the rest of the week. That's why I've got a few sugar-free desserts still in the freezer. I like them, but I don't eat sweets often, with or without sugar."

I picked up my coffee cup. "If Angelica made them, they're delicious. I wonder—do you have any creamer for the coffee?"

Jessa jumped to her feet. "I'm sorry! I've been so scattered since Mom died."

"Understandable. It's a hard time." I don't like creamer, but it was a good excuse to get her out of the room.

While she ran back to the kitchen, I scooped a generous forkful of the fluffy, creamy pie into one of the small plastic bags I'd taken from Johnny's stores. Nick might not be on board with collecting evidence, but that didn't mean I wasn't. My coat's pockets were large enough to hold a small meal.

Arsenic, Johnny said, was odorless and tasteless, perfect for hiding in food, especially at the hands of a master baker. I thought of the way Angelica's eyes turned hard when she talked about her restaurant ambitions and her determined pursuit of the first flute position. Would she kill to get her and Brett's inheritances? Setting aside our previous acquaintance and her generosity to Merry, also called marketing, I didn't know anything about her that would eliminate her as a suspect. After all, she married Brett, jerk extraordinaire.

I didn't think Brett could cook anything, but did Project Poison need a master baker? Could anyone—say, Brett or Jessa—insert a little bit of arsenic in each dish? Of course, suspicion would rest on the person who prepared the food, but anyone with access could fatally doctor it. And Jessa had been a sneaky brat in high school. When Nick moved in with me, he was relieved that my sisters didn't play pranks that threatened his schoolwork. She could have improved—I hope I had grown up better—but I wasn't going to count on it without evidence.

When Jessa returned with a pitcher of cream, I was pushing the remains of my pie around my plate. She went back to the kitchen for more coffee for the upstairs crew. I scooped the rest of the pie into another plastic bag.

On to the biological samples.

When Jessa returned, we traded desultory comments about what we were doing now. She would soon complete her master's degree in global finance, a cold-hearted major if ever I heard one. After a few minutes of hearing about her studies and life's ambitions—she looked as flinty as Angelica when she talked about them—I asked the way to the restroom.

"Oh! Down the hall to your left." She blushed. "It's a mess. I've been trying to sort my mother's things, but ..."

"It's hard," I agreed. "Would you like me to help you get started? If you want to donate some things, I can take them to a shelter or other nonprofit. That's what my friends did for me when my mother died."

"Was that long ago?" Her face softened into empathy.

"In college." I gave her a crooked smile. "If you were wondering, it doesn't get better, not really. The pain isn't as sharp, but the gaping hole in your life remains. Sorry I don't have better news."

"Honesty's better than 'time heals everything' and the other bilge people tell you." Jessa pushed herself to her feet to guide me to the facilities. "Mom moved into the downstairs bedroom in her last few weeks, just before Thanksgiving. I moved her things from the primary bedroom upstairs so Dad wouldn't have to see them. Now they're all over the downstairs bedroom and bath."

I went into the bathroom she showed me and took a quick scan through the drawers of the vanity. I pocketed a travel hairbrush and a small comb and hoped they belonged to Mrs. Thornton.

When I emerged, I wrapped my words in soft velvet. "Let's start with the bathroom. It's smaller, and we'll feel like we accomplished something."

Jessa brought me a fat marker and several cardboard boxes at my request. I labeled boxes Keep, Toss, Donate, Don't Know while keeping a running patter.

I rummaged through the bathroom drawers. "Do you want any of the open or unopened cosmetics and toiletries? Shelters will take the unopened ones."

She waved a hand, rejecting old lady cosmetics. I sorted and held up things I couldn't determine. Jessa didn't do much besides wander around the bedroom, picking things up and setting them down again while I cleared the bathroom. She reminded me of nineteen-year-old JD while Dianne and Johnny sorted my mother's things. Like me, Jessa found it easy to pass judgment on many things, once asked. Anytime she hesitated, I put the object in the Don't Know box.

When Nick and Saint wound their way down the tortuous staircase, I handed the Donate box to Nick while promising Jessa to distribute everything appropriately. I picked up the Toss box. I had my eye on some things that might yield more samples.

Jessa smiled, weary and relieved. "Just having a few boxes gone makes me feel more hopeful."

"Glad to help." I edged toward the door ahead of Nick.

Nick looked like he'd fought a war. Saint pressed close to his side. I wondered whether the migraine beast was yet again extending its tendrils into his brain.

"Thanks so much for coming to see Dad, Nick." Jessa took his hand in both of hers and squeezed it. "He's been frantic to see you."

Nick wiggled his hand away. "Jessa, please understand, I can't be involved with this family. I hope I brought Dad some comfort, but I can't do anything else."

Her face tensed. "I understand. Angelica told me what Brett did. You were treated so unfairly."

"Yes, I was." Nick looked like he wanted to say more, but he just followed me to the car.

Once inside, he leaned back and propped his head on the back of the seat. Then we had one of those deep, meaningful, soul-baring conversations we men are famous for.

I went first. "Tough?"

Nick closed his eyes. "Yep."

"Migraine?" I asked.

"Could be." He reached in his coat pocket. "I changed my mind. Johnny handed me some evidence bags this morning on my way out. I got samples of the pie when he offered me a bite, and Dad's hair and some nail clippings from the bathroom."

I called Johnny to tell him of our triumphant evidence hunt. He told me where to take the samples to be analyzed. The lab seemed staffed by people who weren't ready for the holiday season to end, but they put themselves into gear, since Johnny said it was critical.

Back at my childhood home, Nick sat in the truck's cab for his telemedicine call. I threw his belongings from the garage into the trailer. The weather had returned to its typical Texas indifferent winter temperature of not hot, not cold, so the job wasn't painful.

I had high hopes of avoiding my father, but I remembered his involvement with Nick's story. I dragged my feet on the way to his office.

He yelled from his office as soon as I set foot in the kitchen. He can tell each of his kids by our footsteps. "JD, other people want to use the driveway."

"Good to see you too, Dad," I yelled on my way to his office.

"When are you moving that truck?" he demanded when I appeared in the doorway.

I sat on the edge of the sofa-bed. His office, bare of decoration, was the most uninviting space in the house. That might have been the point. No one ever dropped in to chat.

"When Nick finishes his call, we'll load up the last of his possessions and be gone. We came today to visit his father, who's critically ill. Remember we talked at Christmas about why Mr. Thornton kicked Nick out of the house? That mystery is solved." I hated doing it, but I told the story one more time.

Dad assumed his courtroom mask. "And you know this how?"

"Because I sat across from Brett Holland, now Thornton since Nick's dad adopted him, and listened to him tell it. Proud of himself, he was, for banishing his stepbrother and assuming Nick's inheritance. The Jacob-Esau story always appalled me, but this one takes the cake."

"Mr. Thornton disowned his son without ever asking him his story. Furthermore, he sent that son he believed capable of sexual assault to my home to sleep in the same room with my son." My father looked over my shoulder at nothing—it wasn't like this room had art on the walls—before bursting into an angry rant. "Throwing away your child on another kid's say-so? Never hearing his side of the story? I'd never do that."

"True." I surprised myself by agreeing. I imagined his rage.

I surprised him too. He recovered enough to say, "If anyone ever accused you of something that awful, I'd want you to look me in the eye and explain yourself."

I was glad that opportunity never arose. "I don't understand Mr. Thornton at all."

He skewered me with his gaze. "You haven't practiced law long enough to hear all the excuses people come up with. Maybe Thornton would say he was thinking of his wife or affirming his faith in Brett, on the believe-all-victims theory."

I could tell he didn't subscribe to that notion. "I've no idea why anyone would believe Brett about anything." I stood up. "Nick and I are going soon. I want to pick up drinks and snacks before we hit the road."

My father looked away into some abyss where I couldn't follow. "You should leave before rush hour."

I agreed. It's possible to make that statement truthfully in Houston at any hour of the day.

CHAPTER 26

Nick and I didn't say much on the way back. He and Saint leaned into each other. Johnny's truck doesn't have a sound system, that not being a priority with any of its owners. Instead, I listened to the music of the highway: bumps, grinds, mirrored in the clattering trailer (like a Greek chorus), engine symphonies ranging from rumbles to roars.

Back at Gregg House, I told Nick we'd put him in the main house until we could prepare one of the apartments. I hadn't looked at them recently, but I knew a bobcat had nested in one of them. I flicked on a light downstairs to show Nick his bedroom near Dianne's office. With Saint at his side, he hauled his bags into the room. A giant, screeching bat launched from somewhere above them and landed on Saint's head.

It wasn't a bat but something worse: Godzilla the naked Sphynx cat, defending his territory, which is everything within his sight. Saint, too well-trained to do anything else, crouched on the floor and pawed at the creature on top of him. Nick dropped to cover as much of Saint as he could and pried each cat foot loose. No sooner had he removed one than it found another place to dig in.

I snatched a spray bottle of water from a nearby table in the hall—necessary in a cat-infested house. I squirted the pile on the floor while hollering, "Dianne!"

Godzilla loosened his claws in astonishment. Still holding my coat, I used it to scoop him up and send him flying onto the bed. When he crouched to spring toward Saint a second time, I sent a long stream of water right into his face. He scampered across the bed, howling, and launched into the air, bouncing on the headboard and then higher to the pendant lamp that hung over the nightstand.

Dianne arrived to find Nick still sheltering Saint on the floor and looking for claw wounds. Godzilla hung from the pendant lamp's pleated shade with his back feet scrabbling on the glass-top nightstand. He lost his purchase and crashed to the floor, slicing the lamp shade as he went.

"Madre de Dios." She stepped around Nick and Saint to collect Godzilla. "Are you ever going to learn how to handle a cat, JD?"

"Not that one," I vowed. "Nick, Godzilla hates men, dogs slightly less. It's best to stay out of his way."

Dianne stepped by Saint and Nick again, her eyes widening as Godzilla dug his claws into her shoulder. "I'll put him in my office. Chantal left her sweater there, and he can sleep on it. He misses her when she's away at her singing gigs."

"Can I keep the bedroom door shut?" asked Nick as he staggered to his feet. "I'll leave Saint here."

"Sure."

But Saint whined in protest, not wanting to leave Nick. Dianne promised to confine Godzilla while they were in the house. Nick limped down the hall toward the kitchen, and I detoured up the stairs to dump my things and see my cat Havoc. She's never scratched, bitten, or otherwise caused me any pain whatsoever.

She let me know how insulted she was to be abandoned with all her bratty kittens. She swore no one had fed her, ever. I crooned to her while she purred and the kittens ran up and down my legs. It was good to be home. I put her favorite food in a bowl and promised to be back after my own supper.

The next day was New Year's Eve. Being Friday, that meant Johnny would prepare dinner for as much of the town as wanted to show up. Since college, he'd prepared a feast at the end of the week to help him decompress. When he began exploring his Jewish roots, Friday night dinner became Shabbat dinner. Beauchamp didn't care. The food was free. The bread was good.

When I approached the kitchen to receive my orders for food prep, Dianne and Nick were arguing in Spanish about the best way to prepare tamales. Dianne prepared them for me during our freshman-year love. She wouldn't thereafter, because it's hard work, especially in a dormitory or college rental kitchen. But here she was in tamales up to her elbows and arguing family recipes with Nick. He lamented not having banana leaves to make pasteles.

When he could get a word in edgewise, Johnny asked about cooking at the fire station for multiple diets. He also had questions about the Puerto Rican dishes he was trying to make in Nick's honor.

We would be treated to, in addition to Jewish challah and Latine tamales, dishes of arroz con gandules (both vegetarian and not) and tembleque. The first I translated as "rice and peas," which sounded bland. Then I saw tomato sauce, olives, and spices go into the mix as well. Tembleque is a dessert, kind of a coconut pudding.

No one seemed to need me for anything. I volunteered to make margaritas in the spiffy machine my old law firm gave me when I resigned to move to Beauchamp.

Dianne made a face. "You always use enough tequila to strip paint."

Nick gazed from her to me. "How about I fix some real, authentic daiquiris, not the sweet peach and strawberry trash, but the original, with limes?"

All I could do was join the chorus of approval. After I gathered ingredients and showed Nick how to work the margarita machine, I turned to Dianne. "Can I do anything?"

"Yes. We're having uvas suertes. You can count twelve grapes into each of these margarita glasses." Dianne gestured to a bag of plastic glasses on the dining room table next to a bag of green grapes. "We're inviting the dinner guests and the neighbors to count down to the new year with us. Everyone needs a glass of grapes to eat in the first minute of the new year."

Nick pretended astonishment. "Heresy! You eat them in the last minute of the old year."

While they laughed through their argument, I sat down with the grapes and glasses. This task was about my speed.

Zap and Merry sent a selfie of themselves eating a LED-candlelit dinner and toasting each other with the hospital's grape drink in Merry's hospital room. I hadn't seen anything that romantic in far too long. They sent another, slightly wavy from being shot through the NICU window, of Merry with Jadey. Merry's broad smile was enough of a progress report.

When Dianne passed by me, I tapped her on the arm and showed her the photo of Zap and Merry. "What do your parents think about Merry? Specifically, Zap and Merry?"

"They love Merry. They've known her since she was ten." She turned thoughtful. "I think they'd welcome her into the family with open arms. And if they did not, I would convince them. I'll say that Zap has yearned for Merry since she was in high school, and he should not have to serve seven years for her, like Jacob did for Leah in the Bible."

She convinced me. "Biblical references always work."

We had no more time to talk because our neighbors poured in for dinner, which garnered verbal praise and more importantly, disappeared like a plague of locusts had descended on it. People wandered in and out of the house all evening, with a big surge at 11:00 as we set up Multi-ABBA unplugged (minus our soprano Chantal, who had a New Year's Eve gig in Austin). The gallery-hall filled to the point I thought the walls were stretching.

I watched the daiquiri level go down, down, down with a sigh. I'd been taught not to drink alcohol before or during a gig, "taught" being a euphemism for "threatened with bodily harm." With a sigh, I accepted a cup of hot chocolate from Dianne and added an extra peppermint stick to console myself. Spoiler: it did not.

Dianne suggested that we perform some Lin Manuel Miranda music in honor of his and Nick's Puerto Rican roots.

Nick's eyes lit up. "How about 'Helpless' from *Hamilton?*"

Not being a soprano, Dianne settled on "You're Welcome" from *Moana.* We play enough quinceañera gigs (thanks to her mother) that we always have a few songs ready for the kiddies. *Moana, Encanto,* and

Coco go over well. As Dianne pranced about, singing in her rich, chocolatey voice, I could almost see feathers and scales, though Quetzalcoatl was not the song's deity.

After that, we played the highest energy ABBA songs we knew, starting with "Waterloo." In the last song before the New Year's tunes, Dianne led the crowd up and down the gallery-hall while bellowing "I Am the City." After a few repetitions, I could play it in my sleep.

On her last trip up, she twirled and draped my right arm around her while I pounded the bass line with my left hand. When she pulled me away from the piano and led my steps into the kitchen, Johnny realized it was all up to him. He drove the bass line as hard and loud as he could with an unamplified U-bass. I got to dance for 32 bars that night. A musician's life is hard.

We ended the set with ABBA's "Happy New Year" while some guests ate grapes in the last minute of the year. We went on to "Auld Lang Syne" for those who ate their grapes in the first minute of the new year. I didn't do either, since my fingers were on the piano keyboard.

Before the last chord shimmered into silence, I darted toward the kitchen in hopes of claiming a daiquiri.

The margarita machine was clean and retired for the night. I wanted to cry.

Nick appeared at my shoulder with a mega-super-grande cup from a local restaurant. "Dianne said to save you a daiquiri."

I gazed on the slush-filled cup with delight and sorrow. "Do you want to split it?"

"Nah, you take it."

That much drink, even with a minimum amount of rum, would knock me flat. And Dianne would throw me out.

Some people might have poured out part of the drink. Not in my nature.

I bid the room farewell and took my drink upstairs to nurse it. The sound system blasted out "Sin Salsa No Hay Paraiso" from (of course) Puerto Rico. Nick was going to feel so welcome he'd never leave. My last glimpse of downstairs was Nick and Dianne, hips flying, dancing a half inch apart.

I settled in bed to talk to Havoc and her four kittens. She understood. The kittens didn't, but I fell asleep rather than explain to them. Was I drunk? How would I know?

CHAPTER 27

Since we're not a sportsball house, New Year's Day was a comatose affair. Dianne had already set off for San Mateo by the time I yawned myself out of bed to attend to the cats. Whew! She wouldn't see me hungover, not that I was.

She took Mrs. Ly and my grandparents too. Mrs. Ly would make one last visit to Merry to make sure all was well medically. My grandparents would stay with Merry while they waited for Cherry to return. Dianne would take Zap to catch the train to Dallas because he had to work on January 2. After lunch, she'd take Mrs. Ly back to her apartment in her seniors' community in Austin.

We kept busy the next few days, fixing one of the backyard apartments for Nick. He chose the last one in the row of four efficiencies, the furthest from our intern's place, to give them both more privacy.

That unit needed the most work. Acknowledging that Nick had the actual skills, I cleaned up after the bobcat. Saint found that part fascinating. He and Nick would spend a few more days in the main house to let the bleach, purple stuff, and enzyme cleaners air out.

Besides, Nick wanted to buy a new bed that he'd take when he moved. It would take a few days to be delivered. At least he now looked beyond the next ten minutes and made plans.

When we staggered in the main house for lunch that day, Nick declared our efforts complete, with nothing left to do but watch the paint dry.

With Dianne at a networking lunch hosted by local bankers, only Johnny joined us for lunch. The amount of holiday leftovers being thin, I added my signature meal of tomato soup and grilled cheese sandwiches.

Johnny handed out printouts from the lab to Nick and me. "They did this quickly, even for a rush job."

I blinked at the squiggles on the page, which might have been Japanese for all I understood. Okay, not fair. I read the numerals. I just couldn't translate them. "Explain it to me like I'm five, Johnny."

"These two people ate low doses of arsenic regularly for months, according to the information in their hair. One pie sample also contained arsenic. The tap water showed no significant amount. Perfectly safe to drink, if that's possible."

A pit in my stomach grew to Grand Canyon size. "They had family dinners every Sunday. Brett and Angelica brought desserts, big enough for the parents to eat for the rest of the week. Sugar-free for mother, sweetened for father."

Nick flinched. "But Jessa lives there too. Is she showing symptoms?"

My stomach churned. "I didn't notice any. But she doesn't eat sweets and spends most of her time at school and at work. She gave me a piece of sugar-free butterscotch pie because she'd taken the last sugary piece to Mr. Thornton."

"Something she would say, if she poisoned the desserts," Johnny observed. "The butterscotch pie didn't contain arsenic. That implies a different target than the diabetic mother."

Nick didn't look any better than me. "But my stepmother ate the poisoned stuff anyway. I wish I hadn't dated a murderer."

"Angelica wasn't a murderer in high school." I felt queasy, remembering I'd eaten several of her meals.

"Angelica made the desserts? That is a fact?" Johnny helped himself to the last of the arroz con gandules, vegetarian version.

Nick scowled. "Brett couldn't make a PBJ sandwich."

Johnny's mouth opened in amazement. "Really? Is he mentally handicapped?"

"Just a jerk. He'd ask his mother or Jessa to make whatever he wanted to eat. Jessa figured out she didn't have to wait on her brother." Nick shook his head. "The screaming that went on in that house. Sometimes I'd lie awake in your house to enjoy the silence, JD."

"We're assuming someone baked the arsenic in the food. If it were added later, that brings Jessa and Brett back in as suspects." Johnny put a vegetarian tamale on his plate. "What would be their or Angelica's motive?"

"There's no saying whether they feel injured or resentful." I started on my second grilled cheese sandwich. "But money's always high on the list of motivations. If Mr. Thornton inherited enough to rebuild his father's house, he's wealthy enough to tempt anyone."

"I can't help noticing that I have the best motive of anybody." Nick's expression turned gloomy. "Both being wronged and needing money."

"That's bound to come up," I agreed. "Your opportunity seems limited, though. How would you have regular access to their food?"

Johnny considered the matter. "I'm sure there's a way Nick could have done it, though including Angelica's grandparents might be harder."

"I'm not half that clever," protested Nick.

"I'm sure it wouldn't be beyond you if you had sufficient motivation," Johnny assured him.

Nick squirmed at Johnny's idea of comfort.

Johnny didn't notice. "The situation is critical, given that Nick's father is alive but ill. JD, what course of action do you suggest? Should we inform the police?"

I frowned. "The way we obtained our samples might not stand up enough for a court order to exhume Crystal. Sure, Nick and I were given pie. Jessa gave me her mother's hairbrush and other toiletries, but Nick's father didn't give him hair or fingernails. Mr. Thornton needs to be tested for arsenic poisoning. How we make that happen is another question."

Nick clutched the edge of the table until his fingers turned white. "I'll call him, tell him I'm concerned with what I saw and suggest he ask his doctor to do some tests."

"You'd do that?" I leaned my chair back on two legs. "I thought you didn't care."

"I don't, but it seems the course of action least likely to raise suspicion. We don't want to tip off the murderer. JD, if I can run into a burning building, I can talk to my father." He looked brooding and lofty, like the hero he was. "And I'd better do it now, before you and I talk me out of it."

I looked at Johnny. "I agree we need to keep a low profile."

Nick pushed himself to his feet with force and marched down the gallery-hall. Saint followed close behind, his nails clicking on the wooden floor. He placed the call and put the phone to his ear as he paced to and fro. When he faced my direction, I saw his Adam's apple rise and fall with multiple swallows.

He'd reached the front door when someone picked up on the other end. I couldn't hear the standard greetings.

"Dad, I'm worried about you. I'm an EMT, and I shared my concerns with another medical professional."

I grinned at the other "medical professional," who accepted the tribute without reaction. Vets are medical personnel, after all.

"He thought a test for heavy metals, such as arsenic, would be a good idea." He paused after each sentence. "Well, arsenic can be in the water. If your test is positive, you can ask the city to test your water. If you like, I'll set up a three-way call with your doctor and explain my concerns."

For somebody who didn't care, Nick surely dove deep. He reached the far end of the hall again. The pauses grew longer, and I couldn't make out all the words. I grew impatient until he returned to the kitchen end of the house again.

"I understand, Dad. Sure. Don't worry about it." He returned his phone to his jacket pocket. As he dropped into his chair, he made a disgusted sound, something between a snort and a growl. "He said Jessa makes all his care decisions. She has medical power of attorney. Is that the right term, JD?"

"Yep." My stomach sank. So many opportunities to harm the one in her power!

Nick clenched his fists. "He just wants the pain to stop, not particular how that happens."

"Jessa's a suspect." Johnny stood to clear the table. He took the remaining food after offering Nick a last chance at it.

I helped, sighing as I swept up the plates and cutlery. "I'll talk to her in my most official sounding voice. If worst comes to worst, I can claim to be Johnny's representative. He had suspicions and ran these tests, and now it's up to her to confirm them medically."

Nick scowled. "What if she refuses?"

I spread my hands. "I'm not sure. I'll talk to a criminal law specialist about exhuming Crystal."

"I can't believe Jessa would murder anyone. She was a pain, and she hung around with mean girls, but she wasn't bad herself." Nick slumped in his seat. "Angelica either."

I blocked the image of her lovely face. "Can't you? Have you ever known anyone more determined than Angelica? She was a barracuda in band, and she already knew the career she wanted then. The Thornton inheritance could spiff up her grandfather's restaurant. It needs it."

Nick didn't look at me. "You said her grandparents had the same symptoms."

I spun my imaginary tale. "Say she's tired of waiting for the restaurant to be hers, tired of arguing with Granddad about everything. Maybe they have insurance money that would come in handy. Angelica's worked hard, and restaurant work isn't that profitable."

Saint nudged Nick's thigh, and Nick leaned over and hugged him. "She did marry Brett. Maybe they're birds of a feather. And Jessa's not any less ambitious than Angelica. Brett, I'd believe anything about him."

No one spoke as we stared at the empty table. At some point, Dianne returned and called from the kitchen. "Would anyone like to split the last of the tembleque with me? There's rice pudding too."

None of us wanted dessert. Nick looked as queasy as me. We might have invented a new diet: treat all sweets like they contained arsenic.

CHAPTER 28

I set up a video call with Jessa an hour later. Nick and Johnny were in my office with me, but out of her line of sight.

We did the civility dance, asking after each other's health, before I plowed in.

"I hope you don't mind my asking your father's diagnosis when you took him to the ER."

"Are you asking for Nick? Daddy didn't tell him?"

"That's right." I snapped at the excuse.

Nick looked up at the ceiling with a sigh. He mouthed. "I don't care." That statement conflicted with his presence in the room.

Jessa pulled at her ponytail. "It's so frustrating. They don't know why he's having these gastric attacks. They just treat the symptoms and hand me words that mean 'We have no clue.'"

Now came the sticky part. "As an EMT, Nick was concerned and discussed the case with my partner, who's with the Alvarez County Justice of the Peace. From your father's appearance in the photo, he suspects long-term arsenic poisoning."

Jessa's face went ashen. She opened her mouth several times, but nothing came out. From the corner of my eye, Johnny watched her reactions with clinical ferocity. Angelica wasn't the only one who could have poisoned the desserts. If Jessa brushed me off—

"How?" she croaked. "Should we get the water tested?"

"First get him tested. It's a quick test. We'll figure out where to go from there."

She scoffed, "It may be a quick test, but getting the medical team to do it fast is a whole nother game. I'll call right now."

"Let me know how it goes. If it would help for my partner to talk to the doctor, he will."

Johnny looked nonplussed.

"I will." She bit her lower lip. "I know Nick really does care."

I agreed and signed off before Nick exploded. I tried to soothe him. "Look, if her believing that keeps us in the loop without having to admit we surreptitiously collected evidence, go with it. You've already told her you never want to see the family again."

His face flamed as red as Jessa's hair. He growled and flung himself out of my office. "Walkies, Saint!" he called in a sweeter tone. The front door opened and shut hard seconds later.

Then came the waiting. I imagined many roadblocks, some nefarious, some bog-standard bureaucracy, as in unwilling doctors or insurance companies.

A distraction arrived in a surprising form. Since no one was at the front desk, I walked out of my office when I heard the front door open. Seeing Mallory Mason gave me a start. I looked around for help, to no avail.

"Um, hi?" That's me, wordmeister.

"Hi. I'm on my way home from Houston. I have to work tomorrow. Are Merry and Jade still doing well?"

"Last I heard, yes." I glanced at my phone to be sure. Belatedly, I gestured to the cluster of chairs around the fireplace.

"I tried to get your father to go see her again. He does love his children. I thought he should show it by appearing in their lives more." She sat in the red throne chair. It suited her. "I haven't had a chance to talk to you over the holidays, and I hoped I would."

"Oh?" I said, full of repartee as I lowered myself onto the sofa. Her smile used to charm me from head to toe and all parts in between. What happened? Besides her falling hard for my father while keeping me at an arm's length.

"Yes, I didn't know if I'd be at any more family events. Your father and I won't be taking our relationship to the next level—or any level."

"Ah?" My cleverness astounds me sometimes. "I'm sorry" stuck in my throat, but I managed, "Without you, he wouldn't have given us real Christmas presents. He wouldn't have come to San Mateo to be with Merry when she gave birth. You've been good for him."

"I'm glad. But he needs to be good for me too." She looked away. "What happened to him, JD? He's so wounded."

I understood now why she hadn't wanted to room with him in San Mateo, even though she'd acted as his hostess for Christmas. I ruminated, hoping I didn't look like a cow. "They—the grandparents and other family—said he never got over my mother dying of cancer, but I never bought it. Mother fell sick when I was fourteen and died when I was nineteen. I didn't like him before then either."

The silence lay between us like a soaked weighted blanket. At last Mallory burst out, "He could have been—he could have been you."

I jerked upright, like she poked me with a taser.

She focused on the floor. "He hates everything you love, though he used to do it. Now he's scornful of poetry, literature, music—"

I scowled. "Me."

She flushed but wouldn't look in my direction. "He seemed so much like you when I met him. When the new wore off, it was hard to listen to him. My job as a librarian is to preserve culture and open its doors to the world. I could tell he thought my work didn't matter."

I noticed she skimmed by my remark. "My mother worked at the school library. Her work didn't matter either. I'm not sure anybody's work matters but his. I wonder what he'll do when he retires."

"He has no intention of retiring. He wants to work until he drops."

"Sounds like pure hell to me, but totally like my father. He makes work his life and never has to think about having a life. I hope my mother found happiness with him." I shut up before my voice betrayed me.

"That's sad." Her voice broke.

I didn't know what to say. Someone had pressed the Puree button on my emotional system.

Crystals of revelation dropped and glittered: No wonder my father hated my move to Beauchamp and the Black Orchids. I completely abandoned the path he'd trod, the path he'd dedicated his life to.

A month ago, my heart would have leapt at Mallory's implied admiration, but now it stayed steady, with a soupçon of sadness for my father, for her, for me, for the couples who would never be, for the crush that had withered on the vine. I glanced down at her. She looked tired and fragile. For the first time ever, she looked older than me.

I didn't realize how long I'd sat weltering in my thoughts until I heard a chuckle with mirrored sadness from her.

"Don't worry. I still can't see me with a twenty-something, even one as attractive as you."

"I'm not sure what I should say. Could you just imagine that I said it?" I didn't want to change her mind, but I didn't want to look overjoyed either.

"I'll do that." She sounded amused as she rose. "But if friendship is still on the table, I hope you'll stop by on your way to or from immigration court in Pearsall."

"I will. I look forward to it." I hurried forward to close the door behind her and shut out the cold.

I kept myself to myself that night, mulling over relationships and contradictory emotions while playing with Havoc and her kittens. Soon they'd be adoptable age. I wasn't sure how I felt about that.

Yes, I was. I didn't want it to happen.

Fortunately, before I could wind myself too tight, Jessa video-called before 9:00 a.m. the next morning. She provided the answer we already deduced.

"Dad's urine test was positive." Her face was still blanched, with freckles sticking out like tiny gold beads. "They're testing his fingernails too, but that takes a few days. In the meantime, they'll start treatment. I'm going to get a home test kit for our tap water."

"Good thinking." Her quick actions made me happy and relieved. Her participation in the poisoning seemed less likely. I didn't like to think of my friend's little sister as a murderer.

But that brought us back to Angelica, who also seemed like a nice woman. And I'd been in band with her. Musicians shouldn't do evil things.

But somebody poisoned the Thornton family, and I didn't get to choose the culprit.

Speaking of Angelica, I received a distraught text from her soon after my call with Jessa.

ANGELICA THORNTON

I can't get over what Brett did to Nick. Jessa says you know where he is. I have to talk to him. Could you ask him to come by the restaurant today at 2? That's after lunch rush.

I rapped on Nick's bedroom door. At his invitation, I walked in and handed him my phone. As usual, Saint was curled up next to him. Not so usual was Godzilla pressed close to the big dog. Godzilla looked embarrassed, as though he'd been caught in flagrante delicto.

"It's cool, Zil. I know you love a warm spot," I told him.

He curled himself tighter and closer to Saint, who gave the cat's bare forehead a swipe of his tongue.

Nick shoved my phone back with something between a snarl and a sigh.

I put it in my pocket. "You don't have to see Angelica. You talked to your dad this week. That should give you enough character credits for the next month."

"There ought to be a scout badge for family reparations, extra points for stepfamilies," grumbled Nick.

"That still wouldn't include old girlfriends. Though I'd do an old girlfriend badge before family."

"Speaking of old girlfriends, I'll go ahead and finish with Angelica. It feels like cleaning up. She'll apologize all over the place like Jessa did, but it won't be as bad. I'm so over the girl."

"Let's go early to see Jadey and have lunch with Merry. We can go by the restaurant afterward. Not sure why Angelica wants you there, but it's a public place. She's not likely to cause a scene. Just don't eat anything."

His face fell into sadness, a mirror of how I felt as I imagined Angelica as a poisoner. I wished everything didn't point to her.

CHAPTER 29

I pulled up to Gina's at straight up two o'clock. I sent a text announcing our arrival.

Nick stopped my hand as I reached for the ignition. "Wait. Would you drive around the block? I'm not ready. I need to do some breathing exercises."

I shrugged and put the car back in gear.

While I drove, Saint nuzzled Nick's cheek. Nick patted his dog and focused his gaze out the window during his slow in-breaths and longer out-breaths.

As we rounded the last corner, Nick said. "Okay. We can do this now, me and Saint."

Just as I backed into a parking space across the street from Gina's, the restaurant's front windows exploded. Flames roiled out. A couple of women burst out the door screaming, as though they'd been shoved, maybe by the tall shadow of a woman behind them. Their cute pink uniforms contrasted with the horror of the burning building.

Nick gasped. "Move the car down the block! Do you have masks, any kind?"

I obeyed and stopped when he told me to. "Glove box."

He grabbed a handful of masks and threw one to me. "Call 911." He jumped out to open the backseat door for Saint. "Come on, boy."

While they ran full speed down the narrow street beside the restaurant, I punched the emergency button on my phone and jumped out of the car to follow them. Nick shouted at the figure running away behind the building. The man twisted toward us for a second, his eyes widening in recognition. Mine did too.

Nick cut through the lot across the street on the backside. Construction workers stared at the fire's furore on the front side of the restaurant. Nick stopped, but I kept going, determined to bring down the escapee.

"JD!" Nick shouted. "Help me with the ladder. We have to get the people out of the second floor. Rescue before revenge."

I pointed down the alley and told the workers, "Go get that guy. He set the building on fire."

The workers divided like the Red Sea, some taking over the chase, some picking up the ladder with us. With that many helpers, the ladder stood against the restaurant side wall in seconds. Now it registered in my brain that I'd seen shadows in the upstairs windows. How many? Who?

"Spot me, JD." Nick pulled on his N95 mask—a laughable defense against the inferno, but all we had—and his gloves. "Sit, Saint. Wait for me with JD." Saint sat by the ladder and whined.

Flashbacks of the fire I'd been in a few months ago threatened to consume me. I panted and leaned into the ladder to stop trembling. I forced my brain to separate memory from current reality. I realized with thanks that I was outside instead of inside a building. That gave me a good chance to survive. Nick, on the other hand—

"JD, get up here." Nick leaned out the window. He had to be shouting through the mask since I heard him just fine over the conflagration. "I need you to carry the baby. Saint, stay on the ground."

Saint's whine grew into a low-grade howl.

"He'll be back soon, Saint." I pulled on my own mask. I winced at its flimsiness, but at least it might keep particulates out. The air was growing hot and hazy. I could taste the grit but wasn't sure if that was a fact or memory-twisted imagination.

Most of the construction workers edged back toward their own territory, but one came forward and held the ladder for me. I clambered up, shaking with terror.

Nick held something folded in a sheet. "JD, I'm going to tie the ends of this bundle around your neck so you can take the baby safely down."

He didn't wait for an answer, just handed me the wiggling burden while he tied the tails of the sheet around my neck and tested it. "That should hold while you go down."

I kept one hand on the baby and switched hands as I climbed down. A woman around my age in a pink waitress uniform tore the baby from the sheet, wrenching my arms and neck before both my feet struck the ground.

She sobbed into the squirming bundle. "Thank you. Thank you."

The older pink-clad woman who had burst out of the building with her put an arm around the mother's shoulders. "School and daycare were closed today. Angelica lets the kids stay upstairs."

The younger woman babbled, "The fire! Whooshing out the kitchen! I ran for the stairs, but Angelica—My babies!"

The other waitress continued to translate, though she was shaking too. "Angelica said she'd be faster and pushed us out the door. Ran upstairs three at a time."

"Mommy, Mommy. Look at me," piped a young girl's voice from the top of the ladder.

A ten-year old turned around and scrabbled down the ladder to the applause of those nearby. Her mother shifted the baby to her other arm and clutched the girl into a ferocious hug. She pulled her kid down the street, away from the fire. Now I could see the brace around her right knee. The older waitress went with them, her arms around both.

I didn't know how many people were upstairs, but if Nick had cleared them out, he should be down the ladder by now. Saint thought so too, his howl louder than the fire now. I squinted through the murk, wiping my sweaty forehead as though that would help.

Oh great. I started up the ladder. How would I get Nick down if he were incapacitated? I was surprised my shaking didn't topple the ladder, but my construction buddy held it firm.

I'd made it up only two steps when Nick's head popped out of the window. "It's our turn."

A high voice screamed. "I can't! I'll fall."

Nick put his hands on her arms. I could see him shouting, but it sounded like a whisper. "Fall or burn, Angie baby. Your choice."

CHAPTER 30

Another head stuck out the window as Nick positioned himself on the ladder. Angelica peered out. "Don't call me that! I told you in *high school* I hated it."

I shook my head. People. Fire's raging around her and she's screaming about a nickname. Still, that got her moving. Nick knew what he was doing.

Nick's voice remained calm. "Better to be mad than frozen from terror. You won't fall. I'm here to hold you. Put one foot on the ladder and turn around. I'll steady you as you come down."

I was going to be right furious if he got hurt or killed trying to save a murderer.

My vote for the best course of action was "leave her," but I didn't say it, not that anyone could have heard anything less than a yell. I'd never known how loud fires are until I was trapped in one. The memory poked me with sharp sticks. I wanted to run. Instead, I clutched the ladder's side rails harder.

But there was Nick, being the public servant, even after this slice of the public betrayed him. This woman murdered his stepmother and did her best to kill his father.

Nick commanded over Angelica's blubbering, "Save it for therapy. Put one leg over the window. Look back in the room, not out here."

She obeyed, timorous. "Oh, God! Smoke's pouring under the door."

"We'd better go then. Foot on the ladder. Keep looking in the room. Bring your other leg out."

"You're too close. I don't have enough room."

"I'll brace you. Put both feet on the ladder. One step down now."

"I can't see through the smoke!"

"Don't look at your feet. You can feel when you're on a rung."

She turned around in his embrace. They crept down step by step. Angelica wept, and Nick's mouth moved, soothing words, I imagine.

Saint paced around the ladder and whined.

"Me too, boy." I remained where I was, clutching the ladder until my knuckles turned white, like that helped anything. I swallowed. The air seeping through my mask had turned gritty, acrid. Sweat oozed on my skin and soaked the synthetic fibers over my mouth.

Nick and Angelica crept down, one slow rung at a time, Nick coaching, Angelica sobbing.

She jerked and screeched. "The room's burning!"

Inside my mask, I wetted my lips as flames licked out the window.

"Doesn't matter. We're almost down," he exaggerated.

Her head wasn't yet level with the first-floor ceiling. It wasn't like they'd die if they fell, but try telling that to someone in mid-meltdown. And Nick didn't need any more injuries.

Saint burst into furious barking. That gave me a second's warning. Gasping hard enough to suck my mask into my mouth, I bounded the rest of the way up the ladder in time to throw an arm around Nick just as he slumped.

"Nick, you're pulling me down!" Angelica screamed. She squirmed and flailed with one arm to push him away.

I leaned into Nick, smashing him into the rungs while I threw her hand away. "Angelica. *Angelica*! He's having a seizure. I can't hold up both of you. Let him lean on your back."

"I can't do this!" She moaned as I shifted Nick into a neutral position for both of us.

"Be still!" I panted. Sweat trickled down my face into my mask.

I thought about offering a pat as comfort, but I couldn't reach any socially acceptable body part. I tried for a soothing voice instead. "Just stand still and take some of the weight. We'll wait for rescue or for him to recover. His seizures don't last long."

I hoped. The fire roared over traffic and panicking people. No siren yet. How far away was the fire station?

Angelica wailed.

Below us, Saint barked in a crescendo of panic. I felt more heft on the lower rungs. "It's okay, Saint. He's fine."

"Somebody push that dog off the ladder!" shouted a construction worker.

"The ladder's not rated for that much weight even without the monster dog," said an authoritative voice, maybe a supervisor.

"Which one of us should jump off?" I demanded in full voice. My vote was for Angelica, but I told myself innocent until proven guilty, yada yada. As though Saint would follow any command from me, I called, "Down, Saint. I'll bring him back safe."

Nick stirred and said something. Saint understood, because I felt him move off the ladder.

I didn't have Angelica's terror of heights. If I fell, I'd know where the ground was soon enough. I blinked to peer through the darkening smoke. If only I could see. A deep breath would be nice, too. Sucking through the mask wasn't getting it.

Angelica choked on her sobs. "I can't breathe."

"Mask. Pocket." Nick slurred words through his own mask.

I reached for his right coat pocket.

Nick twitched. "Other!"

I had to shift hands to explore his left pocket. I panted in relief when my fingers touched something. I inched my hand up the ladder rail. "Angelica, I've got a mask. Reach your left hand down."

She gripped the slide rail harder.

Nick flailed his left arm toward mine. Understanding what he was trying to do, I wove the elastic through his fingers. He pushed his hand up the slide rail until he reached Angelica's white, strained hand.

He mustered authority into his failing voice. "Take it. Hold you."

She inched a finger through the elastic strings. He put his arms around her legs, like that would hold her up. But it gave her enough confidence to pull the mask on. She put her arm around the slide rail and pressed against the rungs. Her shoulders shook, but the mask swallowed her cries as the fire raged.

"The ladder's hot!" shouted Angelica.

Was that true? I couldn't tell, but I'd use the fear as a motivator. "We've got to go down then. Nick, put one foot on the rung below." I inched my foot against his.

"Bad. Leg," he muttered.

"I'm bracing it." I held one hand against his leg that leaned against mine. "Lean against my left leg and try sliding to the next rung."

Nick let his leg fall to the next rung. It fumbled a second before it held his weight. I waited until he took partial control over his leg.

"On my count, next step with your other leg, Nick. Five, six, seven, eight." I sang, "'Why did it have to be me?'"

He made it, shifting his weight onto his good leg. He gripped the ladder with both hands.

Still no siren. How long had we been hanging in space? How long could we?

I used my band voice. "Angelica, move your left foot on my count. Five, six, seven, eight."

She did but kept her hands where they were.

Like an arthritic ant, we moved down, one hesitant step at a time. I changed songs to the slowest ABBA tune I knew, "I Wonder," to keep the beat going even when Nick's foot slipped or Angelica jerked. The song's wondering kept me from my own wonders, like whether we'd make it to the ground by next week.

Angelica managed two steps in one phrase. I sang the next line and took my own steps down.

"Now Nick." I kept singing and bracing him. He grew stronger with every step. Angelica still wept, but she responded to the rhythm.

Dancing on his hind legs, Saint was close enough to jump in my arms, when the comforting scream of a siren shrieked above the howling fire.

CHAPTER 31

I kept singing and directing, punctuated by a bellows-level sigh as the sirens pulled close and stopped. The firefighters reached us in seconds, but I'd already put a shoe on the ground.

In the next instant, hands on my shoulders pulled me away from the ladder. I clenched the slide rail hard enough to hurt, maybe slice my hands. I wished I'd put on my gloves like Nick. With more encouragement, I let go and staggered. I grabbed the ladder again to hold myself up.

Other hands reached for Nick. He fell over Saint and hugged him while the firefighters lifted Angelica off the ladder.

I explained, "Nick's had a seizure. He's still in the post-something state."

"Postictal." Nick sounded close to his old self. "I'm okay, Saint."

"That's why his dog is going nuts."

Barking at full volume, Saint tried to crowd the firefighters out of the way. Or aliens. They could be aliens under all the gear. I was jealous of the gear.

I'm blurry about the details afterward. Stretchers appeared. Good thing. Nick and Angelica collapsed, of course. To my surprise, I did too when I let go of the ladder and landed on top of Nick.

"Epinephrine rush," muttered Nick. "Also PTSD. Both of us."

The aliens carried us away from the worst of the fire and laid us down in a makeshift medical station, a tent with space heaters. My teeth chattered.

Blankets dropped on top of us. Nick rolled on his side and embraced Saint, pressing his face into the brown fur. On his other side, Angelica wept. I caught words like "insurance" and "greasy filter," but I didn't care enough to unravel the issue.

A bottle of water appeared in my hand. I had trouble figuring out how to open it.

A nasal voice proclaimed, "An ambulance will be here soon. There was a wreck out on the highway." I guess that was supposed to comfort us.

Nick lifted his head. "I need to talk to the incident commander from the fire station and the police, if they're here. Now, not later. I'm Lieutenant Nick Thornton, formerly of the Houston Fire Department."

His credentials must have impressed them. No one argued.

I'd almost drowsed off when something heavy dropped a few yards away. I turned my head. Brett lay on the ground in an awkward tangle of limbs. Tied up, beat up with one eye starting to close, blood running from his nose and lips, he groaned. He tried to adjust his position, as though comfort were possible.

"This guy started the fire," a nearby gruff voice declared from above. I could see his work shoes and the ends of his jeans.

I recognized his voice from the construction crew. I tried to get a glimpse of him, but all I saw were the backs of three men in denim jackets as they hotfooted away. I assumed they didn't want to answer questions about Brett's condition.

I wondered what they'd been working on. A sweet, chemical smell lingered, like varnish, evoking a ghostly memory of Nick's furniture building. I wrinkled my nose. I'd breathed enough chemicals for the day.

One of the medical attendants threw a blanket over Brett. Another brought over a first aid kit. I closed my eyes. Not my problem.

I opened my eyes when the people Nick requested showed up. Nick pulled off his mask and swung into a seated position to talk to the two officials, one a middle-aged lean firefighter who'd seen everything, the other a solid policewoman who'd seen enough bad things to bore her. They started out with impatient looks.

He announced, "I need to give my statement. At 2:06 my friend pulled his car in front of Gina's Restaurant just as it went up in flames. Something made me suspect arson with the use of an accelerant."

The fire chief's impatience faded first. "Did you see any other evidence of arson?"

Nick coughed as he breathed the smoke and smog. "I hoped for a chance to look for burn patterns, but when I saw shadows of people in the window upstairs, my friend and I borrowed a ladder from a nearby construction site to attempt rescue."

Nick's voice grew hoarse. He drank deeply from his water bottle, finishing it in one gulp.

I interjected, "We saw a man running down the alley on the other side of the building. That's him over there on the ground." I didn't plan to give away the construction workers.

Nick looked around for more water. "He didn't have anything in his hands. But when I was on the ladder, I saw a container in the parking lot across the alley. He could have tossed it on his way out." He glanced at Brett. "I suspect acetone, judging from the smell on the suspect. Others chased and caught him. I confirm he was the man I saw running away from the building."

"Me too. Confirm, that is." I coughed and waved my empty water bottle at the medical attendant on the other side of the tent.

The officials' initial skepticism gave way to interest. The incident commander asked, "Tell me about your rescue attempt."

"I found three people on the second floor, a baby, a young girl, and an adult woman, who'd gone upstairs to rescue them and gotten trapped." Nick glanced at Angelica, still shaking and crying. "The upstairs had been used as a bedroom. I tied a sheet into a sling for my friend to carry the baby down the ladder. When I pulled the sheet out of the closet, I found a container of arsenic." From his right coat pocket, he brought out a bottle with a blue top like those in school science labs.

"Arsenic!" I exclaimed, the only one with the information to make the connection.

Nick enlightened them. "Arsenic poisoning is confirmed in two cases of relatives by marriage of the restaurant owners. Symptoms have been observed in the owners themselves. I haven't touched this container except with gloves."

The policewoman put on gloves and accepted the bottle.

"JD, give them a card so they know how to find me." Nick smiled like one of Dianne's saints. "JD Thompson is my friend."

"And attorney," I added, in case they needed to know.

"Thank you, Lieutenant. We'll look into this. The arson investigator will want to talk to you." After a repulsive look at Brett, the incident commander jerked his head for the policewoman to follow him out of the tent, apparently to confer on their next course of action. A young officer stayed behind, keeping his eyes on us.

Nick laid down and curled up against Saint. "Good to have an attorney."

Angelica jerked like a zombie to a sitting position. Her face rigid and shocked, she scrambled to her feet and staggered toward Brett.

"Angie baby," he croaked. "I'm hurt."

She positioned herself at his side, furthest away from me. Her voice rose from the depths of hell. "I thought the grease filter caught fire. But it was *you*. You burned down my restaurant." She aimed a wobbly kick at his hip.

"Hey!" shouted the policeman, struggling to get by the medical folks and their equipment. They tried to move out of his way, making it harder for him. After he got by, they went elsewhere. Smart.

She recovered her balance and planted her feet wider apart for better balance. She kicked his ribs. Her voice rasped, "You said you wanted to learn to bake to support me and the restaurant."

Nick sighed as he laid down again. "Too bad I'm disabled and can't render assistance."

If Angelica got any fiercer, Brett was going to fly around the tent. She must have had a few kickboxing classes.

I edged away from him, closer to Nick. "Johnny does martial arts, and he's been telling me since college to stay out of fights when a professional is at work."

Angelica found her stance and kicked Brett's shoulder hard enough to make his body jump. "Instead you poisoned my grandparents." She also found her voice, suitable for full opera, and kicked again. "You poisoned your own parents! You killed your own mother!"

I rolled over and sat back on my heels with a heavy sigh. "I guess I should try to help. If she wasn't a murderer already, I don't want her to become one."

"I dunno, JD. You might get hurt." Nick hugged Saint, whining a query. "No, boy. It's okay. Stay with me. I am not putting you at risk for him."

"She was supposed to eat the sugar-free one you made." Brett pleaded in a thin, pain-filled voice through swollen, bloody lips. "Angie—"

"Don't call me that!" Just as the policeman locked arms with her from behind, she drew back her leg further and kicked Brett's head hard, shrieking with every blow. "You liar! You thief! You murderer!"

CHAPTER 32

I was swaying on my feet when the policeman wrestled Angelica away.

"I want my lawyer! JD, you said you'd help me!"

I sighed. Nick raised an eyebrow, funny from a prone position. Watching the medical team carry Brett away on a stretcher, I asked, "Can I talk to her here? I'm not steady on my feet." I sank to the ground again and shook my head to dispel the cobwebs.

The policeman zip-tied her wrists and encouraged her to the ground with his hand on her shoulder. The medical team called him over, probably to talk about Brett, but he kept his eye on us.

"I'm not a criminal defense attorney." I sent a quick text. "I've contacted someone in Austin, and I can sit with you during questioning, but you'll need another attorney to go to trial."

Her eyes bulged. "Trial? Why am I going to trial?"

"Just guessing here, but one person died from your poisoned desserts, and three others are feeling ill effects. As for today, the fire was deliberately set, and Nick and I are here because of a text from you."

Nick had been watching with his wide, intense eyes. "Yes, the text said you had something to say to me. What?"

"Nothing! I didn't send a text. I haven't been able to find my phone all day."

I exchanged looks with Nick. "I imagine your phone is a melted puddle in the restaurant kitchen. If it's backed up to the cloud, the text still exists, but not who sent it."

Angelica clasped her hands over and over. "You have to believe me. I didn't bake any poisoned desserts."

"Mr. Thornton was eating a pie that contained arsenic."

She looked aghast and even more panicked. "You can't think I did that! I don't know how to get arsenic. It had to be Brett! He wanted to learn how to bake, and he worked alongside me when we cooked for his parents. I made the sugar-free versions for his mother, and he—did the ones he baked have poison in them?"

"The last one intended for Nick's father did. Mr. Thornton and his wife were dosed with arsenic over several months. Can you prove Brett made their desserts?"

She stared from me to Nick and wet her lips. "He didn't want me to tell anybody. He said he wanted to surprise everyone later, when he'd gotten good at baking. I see why now."

"Looks like he's set you up. Everyone knows Brett can't make a sandwich, whereas you're an expert in the kitchen." I wasn't having fun, but I needed to be sure of the murderer. If it wasn't her, she needed to know where she stood.

She covered her mouth with both hands and drew in a sharp breath. Her eyes darted around like a trapped animal in a desperate search for an escape.

Nick asked without opening his eyes, "What did he make for your grandparents? Did they see him do it?"

Angelica started at his entry into the conversation. "I don't know. Maybe? Oh, I hope so!"

I took note of her grasping at straws. "Since they're showing symptoms too, the police should search their home and your place for arsenic. Maybe they'll find evidence with Brett's prints."

Nick sat up. "The bottle of arsenic might have prints."

After the medical team evaluated Nick, Angelica, and me, I went to the police station to sit with Angelica while the police questioned her. Nick stayed behind with the arson investigator.

Mostly I advised her not to say anything until her real attorney showed up, which he did several hours later. I left them conferring together.

I thought I'd escaped, but I didn't set foot out the door before one of the police staff handed me a note. I could have kept walking, but old scouting habits die hard. I decided to be kind and talk to Brett.

The police led me to a conference room. The room decor was early institutional soul-sucker, painted in slit-your-throat beige with trim in major depressive brown. I'd confess to anything to be removed from such a place.

Brett didn't wait for the jail staff to finish the slow dance of settling us in our assigned places, across a wide table from each other, him in cuffs. "Man, you've got to help me!" He still reeked of acetone and smoke.

"I can't." I pushed my chair back as far as I could, unable to stand the sight or smell of him, not that I smelled better. That too was his fault.

He cut in before I started my patter. "But I need a lawyer."

"You do, but it's not me. I don't—"

"But Angie already talked to you. Texas is a community property state, so you're my lawyer too."

I rubbed my gritty, swollen eyes. They shouldn't feel this way after the treatment I got at the tent, but few things work like they should. "That's not how any of this works."

"But—"

"Shut up, Brett." I was pleased my courtroom voice still worked. "One: I'm not a criminal defense lawyer. Two: if I were, I've already talked to another person in this case, making it a conflict of interest for me."

"But we went to school together!"

I stood up. I liked towering over him, but at least I was ashamed of it. "Brett, things work differently in the court system. Either hire your own attorney or ask for a public defender."

"Can you send me one?"

"No." I dropped my voice to a whisper. No one's supposed to hear client conferences, but I'm a realist. Most of the time. "I forgot to mention Reason Number Three: I'd have a hard time defending someone who lied to get my friend thrown out of his family. The same guy who later sent that friend a text, supposedly from Angelica, summoning him to die in a fire. When did you decide to burn it all down along with your wife and brother?"

Brett's face took on that familiar teenage mask of "I didn't do nothing." When he opened his mouth to say something similar, I turned on my heel and charged for the door. To my credit, I left the room without punching him in the face. Life doesn't always give us what we want.

Between the fire and jail, I could hardly stand to be in my skin, much less my clothes. I bought toiletries and a pair of sweats at the nearest dollar store. Not knowing if the investigators needed Nick or me again and not feeling like even the short drive back to Beauchamp, I checked into the hotel again and texted Nick about it.

Then I set about removing the fire smell from my body. I wished I could scrub my brain. It felt full of cotton. Possibly soot. Maybe a little acetone, soaking things into a fine state for combustion.

I laid down on one of the beds and wished for improvement of any kind. I still felt grimy, and faint smells from the fire lingered. Was that my imagination? I'd bagged my clothes, used up full-sized bottles of body wash to scrub my skin red and my hair shiny, and doused my gleaming curls with a fruit salad and lavender conditioner. Those aromas just added to the nasal offense instead of masking or neutralizing it.

Nick tracked me down while I was still stretched out on the bed.

He and Saint bounded through the door with a disgusting level of energy. "The arson investigator let me tag along. We can't go over the fire site with a fine-toothed comb until it's cooled down. You wouldn't believe what you can tell after something's burned. We peeked in and saw lots of burn patterns. There was a definite V pattern in the kitchen where the fire started, alligator charring in the woodwork too. I've had some fire science classes, but wow! There's so much to learn. He invited me to stay a few days while he's investigating. Are you going back to Beauchamp?"

"Um." I thought about it—or tried to. "Not tonight."

"The police have confirmed that Angelica's prints are not on the arsenic bottle and Brett's are. They're getting a warrant to search the grandparents' home where Angelica and Brett have been living. They'll have to send the prints to the real experts for an official report, but there doesn't seem to be a doubt."

"That's great for Angelica."

"For sure. I wouldn't wish a murder trial on any of my exes, not even Bernie. By the way, have you looked at the expenses I sent you? For Saint? Bernie's still swearing he's going to sue me for theft." Nick swung the desk chair around and straddled it as he leaned forward on the back. One hand played with Saint's ears. "JD, do you have any reason to go to Houston again?"

I shut my eyes. "Like maybe a friend needs to go?"

"I could take the bus and then do ride shares, but Saint doesn't like the bus. We hear a lot of 'That's not a service dog.'"

"A dog of Saint's size can call himself anything he wants. But I don't mind going to Houston." What else did I have to do? "What's up?"

Nick let out a long breath of air, like a singer practicing vocal exercises. "Dad. Jessa. They apologized for asking me back after promising they wouldn't contact me again."

"Recent developments, I'm guessing?"

"Yeah."

"When do you want to go?"

CHAPTER 33

Nick grinned. "I want to join the arson investigator again tomorrow. That's a job I can do without endangering myself or others. And let me see when my therapist is available. I'm not seeing my family without backup. I should bill my dad for these sessions."

"Be sure to charge him for my hours too."

Nick lifted a thumb in agreement.

Since the new year had arrived, I'd brought my laptop. While Nick investigated the next day, I visited Merry and worked on preparing for my legal new year when she tended her baby. Proud of my adulting, I treated us both to ice cream after lunch.

By then Nick was done for the day, and we headed back to Beauchamp. After he got a telehealth appointment scheduled for early afternoon on January 6, I announced our Houston trip to the house.

"But that's Three Kings' Day," Dianne protested. "You know, Epiphany. When we take the tree down."

I thought the best way to take the tree down was to run a bulldozer through the gallery-hall, but as usual, the house outvoted me. People would lovingly remove and store ornaments, and the cats would destroy what they could.

After negotiations, we decided to take the tree down a day early.

Johnny and I then loaded the truck with the denuded arboreal remains and the leftover pumpkins he'd bought for pennies.

We delivered them to a nearby animal sanctuary. The staff and animals were thrilled. Wildcats love to shred trees and pumpkins, sometimes eat them. Who knew? Seeing cougars play soccer with pumpkins was a highlight for me.

Nick approved moving the holiday, very important in Puerto Rican tradition. "The next day is the start of Las Octavitas, leading up to Las Fiestas de la Calle San Sebastián."

"More Christmas holidays?" I gasped in a weak voice. I would not survive.

Nick grinned. "My mother and I always celebrated those quietly, because my dad was done with holidays by then. But for Día de Los Reyes, you need to put out a box of grass or straw for the kings' horses—"

"Camels?" I suggested.

"No camels in Puerto Rico. Horses. Then, if you've been a good child, the kings leave you a present."

"Would the horses eat pine needles instead?" Dianne gazed down the gallery-hall, strewn with needles from the Christmas tree.

"I'm sure they would." Nick joined Dianne in the kitchen to look for small cardboard boxes.

Johnny wanted to argue about horses' diets, but we quashed his objections by pointing out the horses were metaphorical. Then we argued whether they were fictional or metaphorical.

Nick set out little cardboard boxes full of greenery sheddings on the fireplace mantle. Tradition required the boxes to go under the beds, but modern kings knew better than to creep around other people's bedrooms at night.

Not many things beat waking to a nose boop from your own cat. I patted Havoc's head and staggered out of bed in the way-too-early morning of January 6. First I took care of my own tribe. Then I stumbled downstairs to feed the shelter cats and scoop their litter boxes.

I can't quite do these tasks in my sleep, but I can do them in the near dark. I can fill dozens of paper food dishes by the light from the oven, the refrigerator, and the occasional night light. I jumped when the refrigerator light revealed a silent, still form at the dining room table.

"Dianne? What's happened?" Seeing a wet glint on her cheeks, I rushed to her side. "What are you doing up at this hour?"

Putting her hand in mine, she squeezed as she lifted her gaze. Still holding her hand, I reached across the table to the silver napkin holder. The scratchy napkin not being the best for the job, I dabbed it on her cheeks, barely touching them.

"Tía Valeria says the veil is thin at this hour." Her whisper was as light as the paper's touch.

"Yes?" I hadn't the slightest idea what she was talking about.

"JD, I don't want to be a witch in a broom skirt with a puffy-sleeved peasant blouse, a witch who mixes herbs and oils and talks to spirits."

"Do you need to be?"

She picked up a spoon to stir the teacup in front of her. "Tía Valeria is."

I lowered myself into a chair across from her. "Unless the Official Bruja Manual specifies a uniform, with fines for not wearing it, I wouldn't worry about it. You've decided to become a bruja?"

She found it hard to speak after a two-ton sigh. "Number one: You do not decide to become a bruja. You are born a bruja or not, though you may study to enhance your skills and understanding. All the blasted herbs you have to know, for instance, to be a curandera, a healer."

It wasn't the moment to remind her that she and Johnny tended a kitchen herb garden, brought indoors for the winter.

She lowered her head. "Number two: I only want to find a way to talk about the, the *Other*, without falling back on Church language, like I had to do last week."

Half her face fell in shadow, but I could see tears well up again in one eye. "The Other?"

"I'm trying not to say God here, JD. I want to stay open to possibilities."

I covered our hands with my other one. "I can understand how you'd like to break free of limiting language, but you gave Merry what she asked for: a baptism and prayer for the sick. You'll be marvelous no matter what you call yourself and whatever you wear." I glanced over my shoulder at the framed photos that graced the long gallery-hall.

I couldn't make out their details, but I knew them by heart. Many showed Dianne in costume—for ballroom dance, Guadalupe Day, wild Mexican folklórico, slinky Latin dance, even her peach quinceañera formal, billed as a dancing dress but with so many ruffles I couldn't see how she'd moved, much less danced.

She snapped, "JD, you say that even when I'm in business drag."

"Isn't that a good thing?"

The part of her face I could see in the low light blushed a deep terra cotta. The air seemed to crackle. The conversation might be going places I didn't want to go. Or did I?

She raised her gaze to mine and dropped it like a rock. Her eyes gave an involuntary jerk toward the kitchen island, where the margarita machine rose in lofty splendor.

And that was that. Something that would always come between us, no matter that I'd done as she asked, to never be drunk again. Not in front of her anyway. I rose to my feet and snatched the trays of cat dishes. Cat hunger was a problem I could solve.

"JD, are you okay?" Her voice held an urgent note. "If you say you're fine, I'll throw something at you. You're *not* fine. You've been struggling since autumn. What's wrong?"

I slammed the trays down on the table. The little red and white paper trays jumped, their contents spilling into each other. "Why would I be fine? Besides yet one more fire to endure, my sister and her baby nearly died, and I couldn't do anything about it."

Dianne covered her face and shuddered. She'd been right next to me in the first fire. She recovered enough to say, "You did plenty about it! You assembled a medical team and got her to the hospital when it was necessary."

"And it was necessary because the legal landscape here would give Franz Kafka and Phillip K. Dick nightmares. The laws would have let Merry die in the hospital parking lot, and I couldn't find a way to stop that, even as a lawyer. The best I could do for a medical team was a vet, an injured EMT and his dog, and a retired nurse."

"That's more than the women dying in the parking lots have. And I'd trust Johnny, his grandmother, and Nick before a lot of so-called medical professionals."

"What do you know about Nick? A slobbering Saint Bernard doesn't add to the sanitation." I didn't exactly yell.

Dianne dropped her voice back into the barely audible range. "I know he's your friend. He must have studied hard in his field. I'm sure he applies his skills with excellence and compassion, that he cares about his community and society and every individual in them, that he will stretch himself to his limits to help those in front of him. Like you do."

I picked up the trays again. "The cats are hungry."

Even at a low volume, her voice commanded me to stop. "JD, you did everything possible for Merry and Jade. Yes, they still could have died. You—they—we were lucky this time. Rejoice in that. Next time, maybe not. For now, we dance. Tomorrow we can work on better solutions for next time. I know you will."

"No, for now, we put food in front of the cats." With my hands full, I couldn't slam the backdoor behind me.

Automatic lights flashed on as I approached and entered the former barn, former garage, now cat shelter. I worked in silence while the cats screamed at me for my poor customer service. You're late! The food's awful! And so little of it!

The door scraped open. I glimpsed Dianne as she headed for a litter cart, which contained a trash can, cleaning supplies, clean boxes, and new litter. She shoved it to the end of the row, as far away from me as possible and got to work with the nasty part of cat care.

Eventually we got close and actually looked at each other. For my part, I wanted to show I wasn't ignoring her. Myriad expressions flitted across her features. She said in wry tones, "Tía Valeria says when you don't know what to do, do something."

I turned away. "Smart lady. I suspect she's right."

Dianne grimaced. "I suspect she's right about everything. I wish she weren't."

The door creaked open again.

Nick called, "You should have told me you were taking care of the cats. I'm happy to help."

"This early? What are you doing up?" I called.

"What I used to do as a kid, get up early to see what the kings left me. Guess what? Dulce de leche for me, and a new chew and treats for Saint."

"I'll check mine before we go. If you want to help here, take the other litter cart and start on the opposite end," I suggested.

As he wrestled the other cart to the far side of the barn where I'd started feeding, Dianne said in her breathless whisper that no one could hear from a foot away, "What a great guy. First time a guest ever volunteered for cat duty."

I wanted to impale myself on the push broom.

CHAPTER 34

S ure enough, the metaphorical (or fictional) horses ate our offerings, and the kings left gifts in return. Dianne loved her dulce de leche, and I appreciated my souvenir of San Mateo shot glass.

Our cats would appreciate the freeze-dried chicken treats, stuffed in every box on the mantle. Nick hoped the cat population wouldn't be offended at having to share with other cats. He didn't know all their names.

Nick's help meant we got on the road to Houston quicker, with enough time for a leisurely breakfast before we arrived at the Thornton monstrosity. Saint appreciated his own plate of sausages and whipped cream (not together).

Over the last bites of blueberry Belgian waffles, Nick turned his eyes on me. "By the way, you never told me you and Dianne used to date."

I tried to display insouciance in expression and voice. "Why would I? It's old history. Three times old, and we're not together now."

"You might have warned me off since I'm staying with you both. Not that I intended to do much about it. I mean, Johnny's cute too, but as long as I'm his guest, he's off limits too."

"You could try." Imagining Johnny and Nick together—I couldn't do it. "But I'm not going to interfere with Dianne's dates. If I've got an issue with them, it's my problem, not hers, not yours."

He snorted. "That noble, are you?"

I speared my last piece of bacon. "No, but I work at it."

Nick sipped the last of his coffee. "Must be part of the Old Girlfriends badge."

"Yep. One requirement is for me to watch her kiss somebody else while hooked up to a lie detector. I get extra points if I yawn."

The weird-shaped black slate house with its blazing clerestories made me shudder again. Some people must want to live in a Halloween house all year long. I don't judge, any more than I judge the Beauchamp family who painted their whole house and brick fence medicine pink. But I don't look long either.

Nick shook his head as we climbed the steps, each one a piazza—he'd begged me to come with him. "I don't say they had to keep Grandpa's house as it was. I liked it, but maybe it was falling apart like old houses do. But did they have to replace it with this horror?"

"It seems a natural for a futuristic haunted house."

Jessa admitted us. She looked years older, gaunt, her red hair a messy nest snatched into a hasty ponytail. She didn't even smile at Saint, something I thought impossible.

Both Nick and I mumbled hellos, not having been instructed in Southern etiquette for "Sorry your family member was arrested for trying to kill other family members." So far parricide hadn't come my way.

She turned on her heel to mount the stairs.

As we followed her sagging, faded sweatpants that might have started life as blue, I whispered to Nick, "I could wait downstairs."

For an answer, he held my elbow in such a way that didn't hurt but could at any moment.

Mr. Thornton's bedroom sported the same blazing white and deep black as the rest of the house. I've heard of a color darker than black, though I don't know how that's possible. The random, jagged floor tiles, the accents on the walls, and the duvet, some kind of furry velour, were that color of black, a dark pool to drown in.

The elderly man in the bed looked close to going under, as though the dark velour sucked the life out of him. It hadn't, of course: that was Brett and his steady dosage of arsenic. Judging from Nick's shocked expression, his father had gone downhill since their last meeting.

"Hello." Nick swallowed as he sat in the chair near the head of the bed. "Dad. I hope you're feeling better."

Most of the man's voice had been squeezed out of him too. I could hardly hear the high, thin tones. "Nick. Thank you for coming after I promised you wouldn't have to. I'll try to keep my word this time."

He squinted at me while Jessa placed a chair next to Nick's. She retreated to her chair on the other side of the bed.

"I'm—" I began as I lowered myself.

Nick spoke over me. "This is my attorney, JD Thompson."

"Thompson." The man packed a wealth of memory and resentment into the name.

I met his eyes and kept my voice steady. "Jay Thompson's my father. Nick lived with my family when we were seniors." No sense in hiding anything. Might as well draw the battle lines.

He scowled until he couldn't maintain the anger. He slipped into exhaustion. "Nick, I suppose it's a good thing to have your attorney on hand, but I hate that it's come to that."

Nick leaned forward and dropped a hand on Saint's head. Saint gazed up at him, concerned. "Dad, why did you want to see me?"

The old man collapsed back on his pillow and closed his eyes. "I'm going into a care home, Nick. Jessa's helped me for a long time, but I can't keep asking her to do so. I'm putting my affairs in order, changing my will for the last time. I want to take your and Jessa's wishes into account. Do you need a house in Houston?"

Nick jerked back, surprised. "Not at the moment. Jessa, do you?"

"I'd like to be able to accept a job out of state when I finish my master's." She glanced at her father. "Depending."

Mr. Thornton closed his eyes. "I have this house and the bungalow where you grew up, Nick. They aren't equal in value, but I could leave them to the both of you."

I cleared my throat. "Excuse me, sir. I expect your attorney will advise you not to leave real estate to multiple owners. If you make a family trust to pay the taxes and maintenance from the estate, having a third person to break ties—"

"No!" Jessa swallowed a shout.

"My ... other son ... will receive one dollar, the last one I'll spend on him." Nick's father burst into coughs or sobs. Hard to tell.

We looked away from his grief.

As long as I was driving in the knife, I asked, "Are you leaving Brett with a public defender? You'd be satisfied with such a defense for him? He's been charged with arson and attempted murder, but he could be facing more." I didn't know if the family had been contacted about exhuming Crystal Thornton, but Nick had heard the buzz from the arson investigator.

"Like murder," Jessa snapped.

She knew.

The father answered only, "Yes."

"What else does he deserve?" Venom dripped from Jessa's voice. "He killed my mother and tried to kill my father."

We let the emotion-charged silence marinate. Nick touched his forehead to Saint's head and ruffled his coat.

The elder Mr. Thornton opened his eyes. "I can't make up the past to you, Nick, but I'll give you a better future."

I glanced at Nick. "Sir, you *can* make up the past to Nick. Some of it."

Nick's head snapped up. "JD!"

"I'm your lawyer, right? Let me lawyer." I took both Jessa and Mr. Thornton in my gaze, the special piercing one I use in court to skewer metaphorical livers. "I assume you helped with Jessa's and Brett's education expenses."

"All of them." Jessa spoke a dull voice. "Brett and I don't have loans."

"Congratulations. I'm still paying mine. UT-Austin accepted Nick, but he decided not to burden himself with debt. My father gave him the support checks you sent, and that got him started in community college, where he became certified as a firefighter. A severe accident disabled him and sidelined him from that career."

Jessa's eyes darkened. "We read about it in the news."

I took a second to reflect that they'd said nothing to him at that time. "He now needs to retrain for a new profession. You could help him do that, Mr. Thornton."

Jessa added, "You need to give him living expenses too, Dad, like you did for us. He shouldn't have to work while he's in school, since we didn't."

Nick let out a long breath and bowed his head. "I still have some college debt from my first degree, not much. I can take the classes I need at Texas Community College."

The old man's head rolled in Nick's direction. "Give your attorney a list of what you'll need." His gaze wobbled over to me. "Jessa, give JD my attorney's contact info before he leaves. I'm talking to her later today. I'll tell her to expect to hear from JD."

"Thank you." Nick's words sounded sour.

His father blinked his rheumy eyes. "Jay Thompson insisted I send money for Nick's living expenses in high school. He gave the money to Nick instead?"

I clasped my hands and leaned forward. "Yes, sir. He gave Nick a monthly allowance and invested the rest in short-term instruments, to give him a start in life after graduation."

"I didn't expect that of Jay Thompson. I'll do better this time, Nick. I'll send you money for college as soon as my people can get it together. I intend to split the remaining estate equally between the two of you. Does anyone have anything else to say or ask? I'm tired." Mr. Thornton shut his eyes and sank deeper into the pillow.

Jessa stood up in one brusque motion and jerked her head toward the door. We followed, the only sound being Saint's nails clicking on the slate floor. When we reached the bottom of the stairs, my phone dinged. Jessa had sent her father's legal contact.

I raised my phone and nodded to her. Nick put his hand on the doorknob to leave.

It seemed odd to go without a word, so I said some. "Thanks. My sympathies. All this must be a shock."

"Shock." She spat the word. "Disturbing, yes. Surprising, no. I knew Brett did and would do awful things. I just didn't think he'd ever get caught." Her face softened, and she looked like my friend's kid sister again. "Nick, I tried to tell them you'd never do what Brett said. I tried to explain that gay didn't mean pedophile or rapist. Nobody paid any attention to me."

Nick gestured to Saint to sit down. "You were a kid, Jessa, and the youngest in the household. Of course no one paid any attention to you. They didn't believe me either when Brett stole your babysitting money and I tried to support you."

"That was so Brett." She snorted and turned to me. "Money was tight until Dad inherited from his father. I took a class at the Red Cross, printed and distributed flyers, and started babysitting in the neighborhood. Brett stole everything I made until Nick built me a little safe I could hide in a tampon box."

I eyed Nick with new respect. "Nick's a good woodworker. He built a dollhouse for my sisters and furniture for my church's Sunday School rooms."

Nick blushed.

"Did he? I didn't know he had such skills." Jessa fiddled with her ponytail. "I'm not surprised Brett couldn't wait to inherit from Dad and poisoned him. He couldn't wait for Angelica to get her restaurant either. Her grandfather always intended to sign it over to her, as soon as he deemed her ready. I bet Brett would have killed her too."

"He tried with the fire that was supposed to take out Nick and me as well. I don't think he meant to poison your mother, though," I said. "He thought bringing her a sugar-free dessert would keep her out of the arsenic."

"What a comfort to her and her family!" Jessa covered her face. "I'm sorry. I'm scarcely human these days."

"Understandable," Nick said in the soothing voice he'd used on Angelica.

"Nick. JD." Jessa swallowed. "I know you two hated me when we were young. I was always hanging around, doing what you were doing or making you do what I wanted. I was trying to keep away from Brett. He wouldn't bother me if I was with you."

Nick's face softened, the way I felt my heart softening. "I'm sorry I didn't know, Jessa. I would have tried harder to protect you."

"Definitely," I added.

Nick asked, still in his quiet voice, "Jessa, do you want this house? I never will."

"Oh God no. It's hideous. My mother loved it, but I don't want to live in her monument, even if it weren't full of horrible memories. An architectural magazine featured it. It should sell well."

Nick grinned. "Let's put it on the market as soon as we're allowed. We can call it 'The House from Outer Space.'"

CHAPTER 35

"I could have driven by this place every time I went to work, but I made sure I didn't." Nick kept his hand on Saint's neck as we descended the wide front steps.

"Really? I didn't know you worked nearby. Which station?"

"District 62, off Bissonet. It's one of the bigger ones, the better part of a block. We had a Quint, a medic—me—a Highwater Vehicle, and an Evacuation Boat." Pride dripped from his words.

I unlocked the car with a click of my key. "What's a Quint?"

Nick and Saint lumbered in. "It's a combination pumper and ladder truck. *Quint* refers to its five features: pump, water tank, fire hose, aerial device, and ground ladders."

I slipped into the driver's side. "That sounds impressive."

"It's a monster. Would you like to see it? I have a therapy session, but not for more than an hour. I haven't been back to the station since I resigned." An ache in Nick's voice escaped with the last sentence. He gave me some side eye and changed the subject. "What were you doing, asking my dad to fund my education?"

"Since you declared me your lawyer, I thought I should earn my keep instead of saying things I always wanted to tell him. That might make me feel good but wouldn't accomplish much. It's great he's putting you in his will, but Dianne, our resident accountant, always says money now is better than money later."

He grimaced and focused straight ahead. Saint nestled his muzzle on Nick's shoulder on the hand towel Nick kept handy. "Your father taught me to take it and say 'thank you' when someone offers money."

"He's not always wrong. And, yes, I'd like to see your station." I would have said so even if it weren't true because of the longing in Nick's voice.

A long-buried thrill from boyhood welled up as we pulled into the parking lot of the spiffy new brick building. Its bays, taller than Gregg House ceilings, accommodated the Quint, my new word for the day.

Going to the firehouse! The best field trip for kids, the easiest for the grownups to plan, with Houston stations always ready to welcome the public.

Nick led me into the office rather than straight to the engines. That disappointed me, but we were, on most days, adults. Before he could say anything, people, most of them men, poured into the tiny reception area.

"Nick! Nick's here! Come see Nick!" they shouted.

I counted at least ten firefighters, looking like a United Nations committee. I was glad he'd landed in such a diverse community. I lost count of the firefighters. They kept moving, either to clap Nick on the shoulder or to call in more folks.

They pelted him with questions but never gave him a chance to answer between the laughter and more questions. Saint thumped his tail on the floor and wiggled.

Nick laughed. "Say hi, Saint."

Saint galloped up to each person for a pet, adding to chaos as everyone squirmed around to let him through.

An older voice full of authority shut them up with two words. "Hello, son."

Nick beamed. "Hello, Chief. I brought my friend JD Thompson to see the station, if you're not busy. JD, this is Chief Soto."

Chief Soto didn't look old enough to justify his mane of glorious white hair. He was built solid and rugged, with defined, ropey muscles, like the firefighters who surrounded him. He and they were ready for anything.

The chief leaned over to pet Saint, who said hi with a furious wag of his tail. "We're sitting down to lunch. Why don't you join us?"

"Depends on who's cooking," joked Nick.

"Nobody as good as you, but it's edible," a tall, muscular female firefighter tossed back at him.

As the crew headed for the dining hall, the chief said to Nick, "I'm glad you stopped by. I received a letter for you, but I didn't know where you'd gone. Things didn't work out with Bernie?"

A shadow blanketed Nick's face. "No. He didn't want me to go to North Carolina with him. I'm moving in with JD instead for a while. I plan to take classes at Texas Community College to become an arson investigator."

"Do you now? We could use an arson investigator. If you'd like to come back after you finish your training, let's talk about it." He opened the door to his office and went to his desk.

He pulled a letter out of the top right drawer and handed it to Nick.

Nick went white and leaned against the wall. Saint nestled up beside him. "Thank you, sir. It's from ... I think it's from ... my mother."

"Would you like to stay in my office and read it?"

"Thank you, sir. I'd rather have lunch with the station now. I'll save it for later." With a last longing look at the battered envelope, he shoved it into his coat.

The station kitchen rivaled Johnny's. The food did too. The cook said it came from Nick's recipes, and Nick promised to send new vegetarian recipes from Johnny. When the meat eaters groaned, Nick said he'd include my tips for meat-spiking any vegetarian dish.

After lunch Nick gave me a tour, like he'd done for many children. The rest of the station tagged along to mimic the worst of those clients. We were all laughing by the time we'd crawled over the equipment and inspected the firefighters' quarters, a great place to hang out.

More high school kids should take firehouse tours and see what kind of TV, gym, and gaming setups could be theirs, along with excellent food. In exchange they'd guard the community while riding fire trucks. And boats!

A siren shrieked, and my new friends were in their trucks and gone before silence fell. The mirth faded from Nick's face as his eyes followed the engines away. I wondered if he'd ever get over the yearning.

Maybe he didn't have to. I asked, "You've decided to become an arson investigator? That could bring you back here again, just by another way, like coming home."

His features relaxed into a smile as we returned to the car. "Going home by another way is a time-honored tradition on Kings' Day."

"We should all be wise guys and look for another way home. Mine? I quit the corporate legal grind and made a family in Beauchamp with friends. Haven't regretted it yet."

"There can be many ways to go home. You just have to keep looking." With that, he pulled out the letter he'd received from the chief.

I drove to the nearest fast-food place and went inside to nurse a soda while he read his letter and had his remote therapy appointment. With the weather now close to T-shirt temperatures, he wouldn't be cold sitting in the car. He did have a 150-pound dog to keep him warm.

I chose this burger-seafood-chicken drive-through quick-service joint not only because it was close, but to avoid a menu offering beer, wine, and more. I didn't want to argue myself out of just one, just a beer, just a glass, not when I had to drive halfway across Texas.

I was tired of alcohol's siren song, screaming from morning to night since Merry went into labor. It had whispered to me through the various disasters of the fall, increased in volume as the holidays death-marched to the new year. Now it howled in a fully amplified opera voice.

Just my luck. This place, while offering the usual cuisine of grease and pink slime, embedded a joke in their drinks menu: water, soda, coffee, tea, and a magnum of champagne, the latter for the mere price of $150.

They probably had only one bottle on site. Not many people coming in for a burger meal want to upgrade that much. The magnum called to me from the cooler, where it took up space that could have been used for something people might order. I'd be performing a public service to remove it.

Deluded, I am. Sometimes I realize it. With great sorrow, I paid for a soda. Thereafter I could refill it myself and not look up at the menu over the cash registers anymore.

I didn't have to. Its words had burned in my brain.

Maybe I should buy the magnum and suggest to Nick we rent a room for the night and drink up. If I got wasted, it wouldn't be where Dianne and Johnny could see me and throw me out of the house. I wouldn't show up back home until the effects wore off. Flawless plan.

But Nick had never accepted the offer of a drink yet. His meds seemed to conflict with alcohol. Maybe, just maybe he didn't want to sit there sober and watch me drink. I ground my teeth and took a swig of my soda. I spat it back into the glass. The fountain mix was bollixed. I poured out my drink and replaced it with water.

I didn't drink much of the replacement either. My glass was over half full when Nick came in for his own drink. He seemed pummeled but hopeful.

He flopped down like someone stole his bones. He looked five years older than he did a few hours earlier when we reached Houston.

"Okay?" I asked with a lack of brilliance.

"Yes. But I have therapy appointments every day for a week. Just when you think you might be getting somewhere, life shows up. And blows up. Hang on. I need to make this call while I'm thinking about it." Nick tapped his phone. "Hey, Jessa. Sorry to bother you. This morning it sounded like you'll be shutting up the house. Could you keep an eye out for some handwritten letters to me? My mother said she hoped the letters she left for my birthdays and big events were a comfort. I never received them."

I couldn't understand the words, but squawks from Jessa came through.

"No, I'm not accusing your mother. My mother left several years before my dad met your mom. Dad might have thrown them away, but if you find them, would you let me know?" He listened for a minute. "I need to start school first, but I might be able to help you with sorting and packing things. If I can't, don't take it personally."

"Ouch." I couldn't think of anything else to say in the face of all these anvils of life dropping at once.

He ended the call and replaced his phone. "My mother went back to Puerto Rico. Her mother was sick. My dad was horrible."

"Abusive?"

"Not with bruises, she says, but with words. She thought I'd be better off staying in Houston, even if Dad never let her come back. He didn't, and the hurricanes tore up their lives on the island."

"Oh no!" Like any other Gulf Coast native, I'm a walking advertisement for hurricane PTSD.

"She had no hope of returning after that, but she followed me in the paper, once her library started carrying the Houston edition. She wrote to me at the newspaper after my accident, but her letter came back. Then she wrote to the fire station after the paper featured me for the children's toy drive."

"You never received the letters she left for you?"

He groaned and covered his face. "I keep trying to have sympathy for my dad, but it's a workout."

"You don't have to solve it today, and you shouldn't have to see him again. I can deal with his attorney. Are you ready to head back to Beauchamp?"

"I'd like to make one more stop." He picked up his phone at its command. Gloom clogged his speech. "Bernie again. About Saint. Says I'll hear from his lawyer. He's back in town after his Galveston holiday and says I left stuff behind. He's putting it out on the porch."

I made a sudden turn. "You know what? Let's make it two more stops. We'll take care of Bernie now."

CHAPTER 36

Saint responded either to the name or Nick's emotion. Saint stuck his head forward. Nick pressed his face against his dog's. "I don't want to see Bernie."

"You can sit in the car, but I'm getting all up in his face at full lawyer volume."

That tempted Nick, and he followed me up to the pink house at a distance.

I assumed the middle-aged guy who opened the door was Bernie. "Bernie! Good to meet you at last! JD Thompson, Nick's attorney. Do you want us to stand on the porch and yell or are you going to invite us in?"

He didn't look like he wanted to do either, but he did take a step back, enough space for me to plow through. Because Nick remained on the porch with Saint, I closed only the screen door.

A slender, barely legal young man (also with angel eyes) lounged against the bedroom door jamb. At least he wore clothes, though his pants weren't buttoned and his shirt hung open and sagged off one shoulder.

I shook my head. "Now, Bernie. You've been saying Nick stole Saint, and you want to be reimbursed for the cost. Nick has borne Saint's expenses since he arrived—a Saint Bernard sure does eat, doesn't he? My forensic accountant is checking the numbers, but so far it looks like a washout."

Exes are always ugly (except Dianne), but Bernie was ugly from the start. He must have charm that he kept for special occasions, like seducing a new boyfriend. He scowled, which didn't improve his squashed-looking face. "That can't be right. I've got receipts."

I countered, "Including the one from the crowdsource effort? Nick's fellow firefighters, little children around the city who'd seen Nick's presentations, and anyone with half a heart sent their pennies—even a few bags of dog food—to help the brave, injured firefighter get a service dog, a puppy being trained by one of the best assistance dog foundations. My, what an outpouring of community spirit! They raised more than half the fee in only two weeks."

"Those crowdsource sites always claim a portion of the money raised, and the dog provider had hidden charges. I wish I'd gone with a provider that covered all the fees, but their wait lists were years long." Bernie craned his neck to yell at Nick, who kept his head down and examined the boxes on the porch. "You remember that! I got you a dog as fast as possible. And this is how you treat me?"

Nick flushed. "I treat *you*? You broke up with me, at Christmas even, after I quit my job to move across the country with you." As his words rose in pitch and volume, Saint stood up and placed himself in front of the screen door. Bernie took a step back.

I intervened. "Gentlemen, let's focus on money, the true meaning of life, after all. This provider, for a certain fee, acquires and custom trains assistance dogs for their clients. Saint is assigned to Nick. He has to provide regular reports on Saint's health and attend refresher training to maintain Saint's skills and teach him any new ones Nick requires. Saint's incredible. I've seen him in action."

"Lazy dog just lies around—"

Nick lunged forward but couldn't move around Saint. I wondered who the dog was protecting.

I held up a hand in Nick's direction. "Saint lies around until he's needed. But again we digress from the financial point. When Saint's services are no longer required, he returns to the provider agency for a new assignment or a retirement home. You can't sell him. And if you say one more word about the $1.98 you might have invested, after the accounting is said and done—"

Nick leaned over Saint to press against the screen door. "Which I never asked for! It was all your idea! I could barely walk or think, and you said I needed an assistance dog. I said to get a dog from the pound and a service dog vest from online, but *you* said he had to be trained to help me. It was all you, because you loved me, you said." He choked out the last phrase. I thought he was having another seizure. He stared into the house. "Who the heck is that?"

"Hi," said the stranger. "I'm Connor."

I leaned on the front door sill and put a death grip on the door handle to keep Nick out. "Glad to meet you, Connor. Take note of all these relationship red flags, will you?"

He snickered and smirked.

I raised my volume. "Bernie, if we hear one more word about any money owed you, I'll involve the provider agency's legal team, who will be happy to make sure their contract is 100% enforced and their dog doesn't end up on a For Sale website. Connor, how about you help us load these boxes? Bernie, you too?"

Connor grinned. "Sure, man."

"I have a bad back." Bernie stomped off to another part of the house.

"Yeah, you have a bad back," shouted Nick. "It goes out any time someone tries to lean on you. And another thing." He made his way to the boxes with Saint following. "*This* isn't mine. This either. I don't know who these godawful clothes belong to, but not me."

He flung the offending boxes over the porch rail. One hit the rail and exploded, clothes and papers flying. Those that cleared sailed into the yard and popped open. One touched down near the sidewalk.

Connor whistled in admiration. "Man, did he do the shot put or something? Bernie called him a helpless wimp."

"He's a firefighter." Call it stolen valor, but I felt pride in Nick's accomplishments and how much of them he'd recovered since the accident that left him near death.

In the end, we each carried only one box. Nick and I were back on the road in minutes, him fuming, me humming a victory song.

"We should celebrate after you do your next thing. We could stay overnight if you want to." I hoped he'd say yes. Surely I could find my way to a bar or liquor store. I deserved it after this day's successes.

Nick punched an address in the GPS. "Dianne suggested we stay overnight. She thought you needed to do something fun and relaxing."

"I ..." What would that be? Let Nick watch me get plastered? The bloom wore off that idea earlier. And Dianne ... Time was, I would have gone dancing with her as the cure-all for any mood. Now I didn't want to think about her. "I haven't lived here in ages. I wouldn't know what to do or where to go. Is there anything you'd like to do?"

"I'd like to go where a lot of people I know hang out. Just for an hour. You can drop me off, but I'd like you to meet my friends." If possible, he sounded even shyer than when he offered to show me his fire station.

"Sure. You've met a bunch of mine."

He directed me to a coffee shop, a shabby affair that didn't apologize for it. The dark-colored, plywood walls wouldn't show dirt or cheap texture, like light colors would. Garlands of sad, stringy tinsel still adorned the walls. Nick led us into a back room, saying, "This room is for parties, but usually they don't have any at this hour."

I'd rather have my party at the DMV with food and drink catered by convenience stores.

A white-haired woman of a certain age pushed through the crowd to meet us at the door. Her face lit up. "Nick! You worried me the other night. Saint took good care of you?"

I recognized her voice as the gravelly, unisex tones on the phone when Nick had his first seizure.

"He did, he and my friend JD." Nick beamed as he gestured to me. "I'm fine now. JD, this is Lin, my sponsor."

"Glad to meet you." I smiled like I knew what a sponsor was. Had I wandered into a multilevel marketing meeting?

Lin handed me a Styrofoam cup full of coffee. I didn't have to taste it to know the depths of its awfulness; it smelled burnt. I sidled over to the refreshment table and dumped powdered creamer into my cup in a vain attempt to make the coffee drinkable. I picked up a couple of red-sprinkled holiday nondescript cookies, the kind nobody wants.

At the podium, a thirty-something guy epitomizing the pencil-necked geek made a bid for attention, shouting above the din, commanding the mob to sit down. Before I could ask Nick anything, he and Lin claimed the last chairs, the folding kind that double as torture instruments. They left a seat for me between them. Rats. Trapped.

"Do we have any newcomers tonight?"

A thin man on the far side of middle age shuffled to his feet. "I'm Glen, and I'm an alcoholic."

The room chorused, "Hi, Glen. Welcome."

A sixty-ish woman, still in Christmas regalia, stood up. Despite her cheerful, ugly sweater, she managed to look bruised without having any purple splotches. "I'm Sarah, and I'm an alcoholic." She added a sob on the end.

"Hey, what is this?" I shifted in my chair. A splinter poked my rear end.

"Hi, Sarah. Welcome," boomed the horde.

Nick leaned over to whisper. "These are friends of Bill W. And mine." He stood up. "I'm not new to the program, but I haven't been in Houston for a while. I'm Nick, and I'm an alcoholic."

"Hi, Nick. Welcome back."

While Courtney, Eddy, and I don't know how many more announced themselves, I sat frozen, my mind whirling like the margarita machine. What an appropriate metaphor. Memories slapped me in the face, first one cheek and then the other. What had I been doing all these years?

"If there are no more newcomers—"

I jumped to my feet. "I'm JD, and it's just possible that I might be an alcoholic."

EPILOGUE

Our drive home was even more silent than previous ones. No music, no talking. Saint cut back on the dog noises. Or maybe I was used to them now. Feeling like a cartoon character whanged by a skillet, I focused on the road. The thin, light Alcoholics Anonymous coin, twisted in my jeans pocket, stabbed my leg every time I moved.

Our phones dinged around two-thirds of the way home.

Nick checked. "A group text from Merry. She wants everyone to meet her in the hospital chapel at 5:00. I hope we can make it on time."

"I hope it's good news." I dreaded hearing something she could bear to say only once to everyone. Would Baby Jade ever come home? What if the doctors discovered some horrible condition?

Nick's silence told me he shared my fears.

I took the backroads to San Mateo.

Nick noticed. "Don't you have to get on I-35?"

I explained, "I-35's clogged during rush hour. I'm going by another way."

"Good day for it." Nick chuckled.

Daylight dwindled on the last leg of the trip. I didn't need a clock to tell me we were close to late. We forced-marched through the hospital halls, now bare. Trees and light strands had disappeared. Tape holding bits of garland remained the only visual evidence of the holidays. Hot cider had disappeared from the hospitality stands, leaving only a coffee aroma to compete with the cleaning chemicals smell.

We were the last to arrive in the hospital's tiny minimalist chapel. The number of religions represented by the barest of symbols amazed me again. The altar was swept bare except for candles on each end. Chairs stood in a circle instead of rows.

Cherry sat next to Grandmother and Grandfather. Next to them, at the front of the chapel, Merry, no longer slumping, perched on a chair. She looked more like her twin every day—that is, healthy. She glowed with excitement—I guessed from spending the day with her baby.

Zap sat close to Merry, her hand in his.

Dianne assumed a shocked Pikachu face. "I thought you went back to work, Zap."

"I did. I came back with my car." Zap's explanation cleared up nothing.

My father had claimed the seat closest to the door. Mallory sat on his right, near but not with him. His eyes scalded the person who took the chair next to him. That would be me.

Dianne had the chair on my other side. Johnny and Nick distributed themselves in the empty chairs around the room. Saint lay in front of Nick with his head on his massive paws.

Zap leaned over Merry and whispered. She shook her head and held his hand tight.

"We appreciate your joining us on short notice. We wanted to tell you our news all at once, while Mr. Thompson was in town." He nodded to my father, whose stiff response hinted his neck might break.

I glanced at Mallory. She might have broken up with him, but I was sure she was responsible for getting him to visit his daughter and grand-daughter today.

"It would be nice to get home before midnight," my father muttered.

I hoped no one else could hear him besides those closest, Mallory and me, but Merry looked hurt.

Zap's gaze grew tender as he looked at Merry, whose cheeks turned rosy. "You may or may not know that I have long admired Merry. Last spring we started dating. We didn't tell anyone because of the bonds between our families."

A gasp went around the room, and Cherry exploded, "Not even me?"

Merry met her twin's eyes. "No, not you. Or the Grands. Or JD. Or Dianne and the whole Cortez family. If it didn't work out, we didn't want a lot of drama. We'd just break up and go back to being friends."

"Think they took a cue from us?" I whispered to Dianne, who looked like she'd just realized how our families suffered from our on-again, off-again romance. Us too, but that's expected.

"You all know about Merry's tragedy at the end of the spring semester." Zap's voice darkened. "I don't wish to cause her pain by recounting it. When she broke contact with me, I assumed she did not want to continue our relationship, though to me, it was everything I'd dreamed of for so long."

Merry squeezed his hand. She choked on her words. "Me too. But I —I couldn't face you. Or anybody."

With his other hand, he brushed a blonde curl from her face. "None of us knew the full story until August." Zap dropped a kiss on the top of Merry's head. "I have spent the months since trying to offer support without forcing my presence on her, while knowing dating must be the last thing on her mind."

"Not the last," Merry whispered. She pulled his hand to her cheek, now wet with tears. "Dreaming of our time together gave me such comfort."

"So brief, the barest of blooms." He cupped her chin in his hand. "I also sought the truth in my soul about my ability to love and raise another man's child as my own. After all, my patron saint did." His wry smile embraced the room.

"Joseph Zapopan," Dianne muttered, for the clueless.

"I concluded I was equal to the task, but again, I didn't feel Merry was ready to hear it. Because of the remote possibility that I might be Jadey's father; I ran a commercial DNA test. I did not tell Merry, on the theory that she knew more than I." Zap removed Merry's hand from his —she'd almost squashed it flat—and laid his arm across her shoulders.

Merry swallowed. "Because we took precautions, I never thought Zap could be Jadey's father, especially when those other guys ... didn't. I tested her DNA in the hospital, in case questions arose later, but I didn't want the results publicly available."

My father frowned. "The legal agreement with the other parties ..."

I cut him off. "We forged that agreement on the basis of their rape, not on paternity."

Zap kissed Merry's head again. "Merry showed the DNA results to me and Johnny and asked us how to read them. I apologize for the deceit, dulce amiga, but I later asked Johnny to compare Jadey's results with mine. I wanted to present you with a confirmed fact, not a possibility."

Johnny sat impassive, despite Dianne's glare. His ability to keep secrets exasperates her.

Merry pulled herself straighter. Her voice rang out, firm and strong. "Zap is Jadey's father. I confirmed it with the hospital today and added his name to the birth certificate. I've never been so happy in my life." She burst into tears.

Zap pulled her to him. Eyes squeezed shut, Merry snaked her arms around his waist.

The rest of us gawked, cried, or exclaimed, as our natures demanded. Dianne did all three. She covered her face with one hand. Her shoulders shook, not sobbing, not at all. She doesn't do that. I pulled her close with one arm, and she collapsed against me.

Zap raised himself straighter, the better to look my father in the eye. I envisioned noble Mexican ancestors lining up behind him. "Mr. Thompson, I want to marry your daughter as fast as possible. She might not be ready to be a wife, but I promise her all the space she needs to heal. Our child will at least bear my name, and I will support them, as is right and proper. I am now on paternity leave from my job, the better to care for them."

"I am never letting you go," Merry held him tighter. "And my father has nothing to say about my marriage. I'm not a cow for sale."

Zap rocked her gently in his arms. "It is just tradition, dulce amiga. I pretend to ask. He pretends to agree. We thus observe the proprieties, but nothing will separate me from you now."

My father sat speechless. I coached him in a low voice. "We are honored to bring you into the family, Zap."

Mallory said something similar in stereo, and he stammered his way through his acceptance. Sometimes I can't believe this guy's ever been in a courtroom. He just can't think on his feet.

Cherry sniffed. "It takes two years to put a wedding together."

Zap grinned, lightening his stern visage. "I know people."

As in his mother, the event planner.

Dianne pushed herself upright. "We don't have to wait two years. We can do something now."

"Are you declaring yourself a priest in another emergency?" That seemed to be a stretch. I sounded skeptical even to myself.

Dianne declared, "I don't have to. You've married a bunch of our friends as a minister in the Church of the Universal Whatever with your online certification. You can perform a ceremony for your sister and my brother here and now."

Zap and Merry hugged each other, rapturous.

My father scowled. "That's not legal."

Typical him.

Dianne declared. "My mother would never forgive any of us if her only son married without her intense participation. I warn you, Merry. I think Zap is asking for a public commitment. Right?"

He nodded.

I added the fine print. "To make it legal, you need to go to the county seat and apply for a marriage license. If Merry's not up to it, Zap can take her notarized statement."

Dianne nodded. "Mamí can plan the church ceremony later."

"I want to do something now." Merry stood up. She looked down at her old sweats. Her shoulders slumped. "But I won't be married in this."

"I brought my New Year's dress to show you guys." Cherry stood up. "I'll fetch it."

"Cherry, I haven't been and won't be your size for a long time." Merry's face sagged as reality loomed.

"It's a shift. It doesn't fit tight over boobs, waist, or hips. It's white with silver trim. It's perfect." Cherry charged for the door.

"If it doesn't fit, we'll split it and sew you in it." Dianne's experience with extreme alterations has saved more than one MultiABBA performance.

My father, still being him, tried to depress us all. "It might be better to wait—"

Merry stamped her slippered foot, still forceful. "I am done waiting. I have waited and waited and waited for Zap, since high school even. I am not waiting for anything ever again. It's too easy for it to be snatched away."

Zap swept her into his arms. "¡Dulce amiga! How I long to never call you that again. Not my sweet friend, but ¡Querida mía! ¡Mi vida! Soon to be ¡Mi querida esposa!"

I spoke in an undertone intended for my father's ears. "They can decide later if they have reasons to wait or if they want to tie the legal knot right away. If they do, we can marry them in three days or less, if we can find a friendly judge."

After some chaos, I stood by Dianne, who planned to offer Catholic prayers and blessings, at the altar-equivalent, once again with a silver cross and an open tome that was either a Bible or a Houston phone book. I mouthed "Thanks" as I raised a thumb in that direction.

Dianne raised her eyebrows as she unknotted her perky scarf to hang down once again in a priestly manner.

"Methodist blessing," I told her. "Our Sign of the Cross."

She gave a quick shake of her head and murmured, "What a day of revelation, this Epiphany."

"I'll say." I adjusted the coin twisted in my pants pocket to make it stop poking me.

Sitting near the door with Saint, Nick extracted his mother's letter from his coat pocket and mused over it. At least the day was almost over. Maybe we could get through the night without any more revelations. Even the happy ones were taking a toll.

Cherry angled her phone to give Dianne's parents in Garland, Texas, a view. Mrs. Cortez wept openly but tried to keep the noise level down.

Grandmother once again commandeered the piano, still shoved in the corner, but with a wheel clamp to prevent it moving. She played rapturous Baroque music with many notes and much counterpoint. I thought I recognized Bach's "Ehre Sei Dir."

Merry glowed in a triangle-shaped dress, Cherry's geometric style, blinged to the max in silver embroidered roses and a feathered, sequined hem. Merry stood at the chapel door and murmured, with a dollop of suspected sarcasm, "How beautiful! It covers my butt."

The dress bore no resemblance to anything she'd ever choose for herself.

Dad and Zap escorted Merry, who leaned on them both, for the few steps toward us. She could hardly stand up in Cherry's silver, four-inch spike heels, much less walk in them.

Cherry muttered as she aimed her phone at them, "You want your hospital gripper socks, Merry?"

I rejoiced in the return of twin-scrapping, one more step toward normalcy.

"I confess I've imagined us in a wedding a couple of times in the last decade, but in different roles," I murmured to Dianne as I welcomed Merry and Zap with my widest smile.

She tossed her wavy, dark hair. "We're not dead yet."

Our gazes locked. Angel eyes. I could lose myself in them.

After we proclaimed and prayed our last, Zap and Merry turned to the room with grins as wide as Texas. They were going to visit their daughter but wanted us to join them for dinner at Boudreaux's.

Dianne and I moved to the piano to play and sing them out with the only logical choice: "I've Been Waiting for You." This time I had no problem belting it out to the rafters.

Thank you for reading! If you enjoyed this latest adventure of the Black Orchids, please leave a review at your favorite online bookstore or venue. A review ranks close to a book sale as the best present you can give an author.

For news of the next publications and other goodies, sign up for the occasional newsletter and blog post on my website at https://dimond.me.

CAST OF CHARACTERS

Black Orchid Enterprises in Beauchamp, Texas

When Devora Ly decided to move to a retirement home, she offered Gregg House, her mansion in Beauchamp (22 miles southeast of Austin), to her grandson. He invited two college housemates and bandmates to join him, and they chose Black Orchid Enterprises as the name of the umbrella organization that combines their three professional practices.

Dr. John Ky (Johnny) Ly, DVM, Licensed Veterinary Acupuncturist, youngest partner of Black Orchid Enterprises. BS from University of Texas, DVM from Texas A&M. Hometown: San Antonio. Vegetarian. Loves to cook. Neurospicy. Buddhist, now embracing his grandmother's Judaism, which she rejected as a nurse in Vietnam. Tenor and bass player in MultiABBA, the ABBA tribute band the housemates formed in college. Assistant Justice of the Peace of Alvarez County (in charge of declaring dead bodies dead) and Beauchamp Assistant Animal Control Officer (dealing with cats and wild animals—do not ask about the wild hog).

Guadalupe Dianne Cortez y Jáquez, CPA, CFE, president of Black Orchid Enterprises. BS and MS in accounting from UT. Hometown: Garland, Texas, east of Dallas. Third-generation Mexican-American. Native speaker of Spanish and English. Alto and choreographer for MultiABBA. Dances ballet, folklorico, and ballroom. Communicates by spreadsheet.

James Daniel (JD) Thompson, attorney at law, mediator. Hometown: West University Place (Houston area), Texas. Double major in pre-law and literature from UT. He and Dianne have made three attempts (so far) at dating, starting in their freshman year of college. Writes poetry and chronicles the adventures of the Black Orchids. Loves Texas beaches, also Paris. Plays piano and sings bass-baritone in MultiABBA. Pronouns: he/him.

Other Gregg House residents, mostly offstage in this tale

Chantal Gaumont, accountant, soprano, bandleader of MultiABBA
    Darryl Swann, intern
    Many, many cats

Thompson family

Jay Thompson, JD's father, an attorney who lives in West University Place in the Houston area. His wife Adrienne, JD's mother, died when JD was in college.
    Jim Thompson, JD's grandfather, a former U.S. attorney who lives in a retirement village in Waco, Texas.
    Arline Thompson, JD's grandmother, Jim's wife, who lives with him in Waco. Pianist who taught her children and grandchildren to play.
    Merry Thompson, JD's younger sister, age 21, pregnant and recently graduated from college with a degree in marine biology. See Book 3, *Family Matters: Lies Across Texas* for more details.
    Cherry Thompson, Merry's twin, in her last semester of college in arts management.

Cortez family

Most of the Cortez family lives in Garland, Texas, near Dallas. Besides her parents, Dianne has three younger sisters and many cousins.

Zap Cortez, Dianne's younger brother, age 25, an environmentalist who works for Dallas Parks and Recreation.

Ly family

Devora Schwarz Ly, RN, Johnny's grandmother, who was a nurse in Vietnam and later for the Beauchamp school district. When in Vietnam, she married Ky Ly (now deceased), who came back with her to her hometown of Houston. She later bought Gregg House with her inheritance. She has two children, Johnny's father and a daughter, both with grown children of their own. Currently lives in Austin.

Thornton family

Nick Thornton, JD's childhood friend, who lived with the Thompsons in his and JD's senior year. Became a firefighter but was severely injured on the job and now has a service dog to help him. His Puerto Rican mother left the family when he was thirteen.

Dennis Thornton, Nick's father, who disowned Nick as a teenager. Two years after his first wife left, he married **Crystal**, now deceased.

Brett Thornton, Crystal's son, younger than Nick, adopted by Dennis after he disowned Nick.

Jessa Thornton, Brett's younger sister, also adopted by Dennis.

Angelica Rossi Thornton, Brett's wife, Nick's high school girlfriend.

ACKNOWLEDGMENTS

It took more than a village, more like a Beauchamp-sized town, to produce this book. I'm grateful for everyone's contributions.

Beta readers: Joyce Casement, Deni, Marjorie Farrell, Beth Helm, Connie P

Architectural consultant: Susan Cory

Book production: Karen Block (editor), James Hoyt (IT & webmaster), Suzanne Waggoner (proofreader)

Fire consultant: Capt. Ken Shoemaker, Ret.

Miscellany consultant: Amy M. Reade

Veterinary consultant: Dr. Millicent Eidson

My Sisters in Crime critique group

THIS AND THAT

One of the nice things about being an author is that your stories can come out better than real life. I feel certain that Nick and Merry will have better futures than those who inspired their stories.

Service or Assistance Dogs

Luis Carlos Montalván, who served seventeen years in the Army with two tours of Iraq, raised awareness of PTSD in the military and advocated for service dogs. We lost Luis in 2016, but we still have his books about his Golden Retriever service dog, Tuesday.

Until Tuesday
Tuesday's Promise
And the children's books:
Tuesday Tucks Me In
Tuesday Takes Me There

Saint Bernards do serve as assistance dogs, but not as frequently as Golden Retrievers, Labrador Retrievers, German Shepherds, and others. Depending on the training needed, smaller dogs like terriers and Pomeranians can also serve. When I was small, I learned about guide dogs for the blind, but today assistance animals help their people manage many other medical conditions, both for veterans and the general public.

Pregnancy in Texas

I would have died before age 30 under the current laws that JD rages about. I'm alarmed that younger friends and family face death and infertility in Texas and other states with similar laws.

At least three Texas women have died for lack of care, and we know the number is higher because maternal and infant mortality have spiked in the last few years.

Rest in peace,
Josseli Barnica
Nevaeh Crain (whose medical condition was closest to Merry's)
Porsha Ngumezi
and those we don't know

PLAYLIST

Follow the link (https://bit.ly/Saints-Play) or scan the QR code to hear the music mentioned in *Stealing Saints*.

"All Too Well," Taylor Swift
"Lawyers in Love," Jackson Brown
"Carol of the Bells," Ukrainian Carol
"Greensleeves," Ralph Vaughn Williams
String Sextet Nos. 1 & 2, Johannes Brahms
Piano Quintet, Johannes Brahms
"Why Did It Have To Be Me?" ABBA
"My Love, My Life," Mamma Mia! Here We Go Again movie
"Mi Shebeirach," Debbie Friedman
"Boat Drinks," Jimmy Buffet
"Helpless," Phillipa Soo, by Lin Manuel Miranda
"You're Welcome," Dwayne Johnson, by Lin Manuel Miranda
"Happy New Year," ABBA
"Auld Lang Syne," The Choral Scholars of University College Dublin, by Robert Burns (lyrics)
"Waterloo," ABBA
"I am the City," ABBA
"I've Been Waiting for You," ABBA

"Angel Eyes," ABBA
"Andante, Andante," ABBA
"Kisses of Fire," ABBA
"Sin Salsa No Hay Paraiso," El Gran Combo de Puerto Rico
"I Wonder," ABBA
"Ehre sei dir, Gott, gesungen," J. S. Bach

ABOUT THE AUTHOR

After stints in professional orchestras, law firms, cat rescue, bookkeeping, and technical communication, M. R. Dimond returned to a childhood dream of writing fiction, which has turned out to be about musicians, lawyers, veterinarians, accountants, and cats.

Sign up for the newsletter to learn about the next Black Orchid Enterprises mystery, or see some previous works:

Birth of the Black Orchids, *Black Orchid Enterprises Mystery Book 1*

The Sphynx Who Stole Christmas, *Black Orchid Enterprises Mystery Book 2*

Family Matters, *Black Orchid Enterprises Mystery Book 3*

Rained Out and Other Texas Holiday Disasters, *Black Orchid Enterprises Mystery Book 4*

Hallow: A Fractured Family Tale, *Black Orchid Enterprises Mystery Book 5*

"Playing It Again" in Hook, Line, and Sinker, *Seventh Guppy Anthology, edited by Emily P. W. Murphy, nominated for the 2024 Derringer Award*

"Be It Resolved" in Riddles, Resolutions, and Revenge, *R. B. Marshall, collator*

"Blessed" in Dreaming the Goddess, *Karen Dales, editor*

"Nine Lives Through Time" in Cat Tails, War Zone, *Rebecca McFarland Kyle and Dana Bell, editors*

"Carol for Mixed Voices" in Best of Strange Horizons Year 2

Find me on Facebook as Madeleine.Dimond, on Bluesky as MRDimond-Author, and Instagram as MRDimondAuthor.

A hard-boiled detective. A beautiful blonde in trouble. What could go wrong?

The aftermath of World War II finds detective Lou Delacroix trying to scrape out a living on the mean streets of New Orleans, harder for Marie-Louise Delacroix now that men have returned from the war. A beautiful blonde with a missing husband begs Lou for help. As she wades through the swampy parts of town full of voodoo, music, and crime, can Lou find the husband and save her client's life? She'll settle for one.

Watch for *The Rude Bird*, coming soon to your favorite online ebook store